DATE DUE

~~2 7 MAY 2011~~			

Demco, Inc. 38-293

First published in the UK in 2011 by Scholastic Children's Books
An imprint of Scholastic Ltd
Euston House, 24 Eversholt Street
London, NW1 1DB, UK
Registered office: Westfield Road, Southam, Warwickshire, CV47 0RA
SCHOLASTIC and associated logos are trademarks and/or registered
trademarks of Scholastic Inc.

Text copyright © Jonny Zucker, 2011

The right of Jonny Zucker to be identified as the author
of this work has been asserted by him.

ISBN 978 1 407 12104 8

A CIP catalogue record for this book is available
from the British Library.

Printed by CPI Bookmarque, Croydon, CR0 4TD
Papers used by Scholastic Children's Books are made from
wood grown in sustainable forests.

1 3 5 7 9 10 8 6 4 2

www.scholastic.co.uk/zone

For Jake, Ben and Issac

1

Danny Sharp gripped the steering wheel as his sleek red Ferrari sped towards the final bend of the Delta Park circuit. The Ferrari housed an incredibly light chassis made of carbon fibre composites, with a naturally aspirated 2.4 litre engine. It spun up to 19,000 revs per minute, with a top speed of 220 mph.

It was a truly awesome Formula One racing car.

Danny could see the massed banks of spectators in the towering stands. They looked like thin multicoloured bricks standing on top of one another. Some of the crowd were waving banners bearing his name; others were pumping their fists in the air and cheering him on. He quickly checked his mirror and saw Anton Le Grand sneaking up on him, his silver Renault ferociously pelting down the track.

Danny felt a jolt in his chest.

Le Grand was his closest Formula One rival. Only one point separated them on the leader board. Le Grand was in first place; Danny was in second. If Danny took this race he'd grab twenty-five points while Le Grand would only snatch eighteen. That meant Danny would leapfrog Le Grand and become championship leader. His body tingled with excitement at the thought of this prospect, but his mind quickly switched back to the race.

Focus.

That was the golden rule of racing. Lose your focus, even for a split second, and you could lose everything, even your life.

The gleaming chrome wheels of Danny's Ferrari hit the bend with incredible force. His front and rear wings generated enough aerodynamic down-force to keep the car on the ground. But he'd misjudged his entry speed into the corner. The car skidded and went careering towards the outside edge of the track. Danny hit the brake with his left foot. With every sinew of strength he could muster, he yanked the steering wheel and just managed to stop his vehicle smashing into a giant advertising hoarding promoting a sports drink called *Action Liquid.* He heard the engine of the Renault screaming up behind him. Le Grand was clearly intending to steal the middle of the track. But Danny wasn't having it. He swerved and took the centre for himself.

The turbulence created by his engine pushed Le Grand back and Danny knew how furious that would make his rival. But Le Grand cut right and a moment later his Renault was parallel with Danny's Ferrari.

They were now on the final straight – a chase to the black and white chequered flag and the finish line. Danny gritted his teeth, pushing the Ferrari to even greater speeds, but Le Grand matched him metre for metre.

Nothing separated their vehicles now except for air.

The finishing line was less than a hundred metres away. Would the power of Danny's Ferrari propel him the necessary couple of centimetres ahead of Le Grand to snatch the vital points? The two cars roared into the final fifty, side by side, the tension almost too intense for Danny to bear.

And then suddenly, all signs of Danny's Ferrari, Le Grand's Renault, the track and the massive crowd fizzled into nothingness. Danny spun round in shock. His mother, Julie, stood by the wall holding a plug socket in her hand.

"I told you to turn off the computer *fifteen* minutes ago," she said crossly, "and as you didn't, I have!"

"MUMMMM!" wailed Danny in disbelief.

"No, Danny. You've been on it for ages. It's a beautiful day. Go outside and get some fresh air."

Danny groaned. He'd been on the verge of a crucial

victory over virtual speedster Anton Le Grand, and Mum had killed the race! He closed his eyes in despair for a few moments, then stomped towards the door of his bedroom and barged out past her.

What was the matter with Mum? Couldn't she see she'd just blown the race of a lifetime?

Danny tutted under his breath as he walked down the stairs. *Power Wheels 7* was his all-time-favourite computer game. He'd never won a series against Anton Le Grand and today had been his best opportunity to overtake his rival. School had broken up a couple of hours ago for the summer holidays and he'd only been on the game for forty minutes. Why couldn't he spend the rest of the afternoon battling it out with Le Grand? There were six weeks to stock up on fresh air.

He stopped for a moment in front of the hallway mirror and stared at the boy with cropped brown hair, light brown eyes and a button nose staring back at him. He sighed. He'd just have to play a bit later, he reassured himself – with the sound turned down.

Danny opened the front door. The sun came streaming in and as he walked outside the warm rays hit him. The sky was a gorgeous light blue; a perfect summer day.

The Sharps lived on one of ten cul-de-sacs in a compact estate. Each road was named after a spot in the

Lake District – like Windermere Close and Thirlmere Close. Danny's cul-de-sac was called Grassmere Close; his family lived at number seven.

Danny's dad, Ed, was crouching down on the pavement smoothing over a tiny scratch on the passenger door of a green Ford Mondeo. A grimy toolkit stood on the pavement next to him; the car's manual was resting on the bonnet. Dad was a postman by day but his true love in life was cars. He bought them, did them up and sold them for a small profit.

"Taking a battered car and fixing it up is one of life's most satisfying challenges," he was always telling Danny.

With Dad's passion for cars it had been pretty certain his only son would be introduced to them at the earliest possible age, and sure enough, for Danny's third birthday he'd received his first toolkit – complete with mini screwdrivers and wrenches. It hadn't been long before he was using *real* tools and working alongside his father. Dad had taught him pretty much everything there was to know about cars: how they worked, why they went wrong and how to fix them. Danny was soon able to talk about carburettors and spark plugs in a way that would confuse most adults.

"Danny, mate," Dad called over when he saw his son emerge from the house. "Can you give this Mondeo a quick wash? I'm driving it to take Katie bowling in about twenty minutes, and when we get back someone's coming to see it. They sounded pretty keen."

"Fine," replied Danny, who was happy to carry out any task that was related to moving vehicles.

"Fancy joining us for a bit of bowling when you're done with the Mondeo?" asked Dad, making his way into the house.

Danny shook his head. Being spotted at the bowling alley with his six-year-old sister wouldn't exactly enhance his street cred! And besides, the one time he *had* been bowling with Katie, it had taken her about an hour to stagger over to the lane with each bowling ball and another hour to choose which drink she wanted. No, he'd stick around here.

Danny trooped back inside to fill a couple of buckets with water. He poured some washing-up liquid into one, grabbed a cloth and took everything back outside to crack on with the job.

Danny started on the Mondeo's roof. When it was spotless he did the bonnet and then progressed to the hubcaps and the wheels. He was a quick worker through years of experience and was just finishing off when he spotted someone strolling down Grassmere Close as if they owned it.

It was Tony Butler – the most annoying boy on the planet; a boy who had been in Danny's class throughout

6

primary school and was now in his form at secondary school. If Anton Le Grand was Danny's virtual enemy, Tony Butler was his real-life equivalent. Tony was a show-off and a mega wind-up merchant. He was also totally vain, so much so that Danny found it amazing Tony didn't have a mirror jutting out from his forehead to give him a 24/7 image of himself. As Tony approached he smoothed down his hair, which was covered in so much gel it looked like a waterlogged football pitch.

"Just the person I'm looking for," said Tony, stopping next to the Mondeo.

Danny lowered one of his buckets to the ground. "What could you possibly want from me?" he demanded.

"That's not a very friendly greeting!" exclaimed Tony, his cold blue eyes looking at Danny with mock disappointment.

Danny sighed. Why did Tony have to be such a first-class pain?

"I'll get to the point," said Tony, his top lip curling. "I know you fancy yourself as a bit of a basketball star, so on Monday, me and my mate Kev challenge you and Carl to a two v two match in the park. Half an hour game; winners pay losers twenty quid."

Danny frowned. He loved playing basketball; he was in the school team and was a decent player. His best mate,

Carl Green, was also in the team and was pretty handy. But Danny really didn't fancy playing against Tony and Kev. Tony was a bit of a psycho and a cheat; Kev was massive.

"Not interested," said Danny coolly.

"Fine," said Tony. "You want to bottle it. I understand. I'll just have to spread the word about you being chicken."

He began to walk away.

Danny felt sparks of anger ignite inside him. Even though he tried to rise above Tony's taunts, they always got to him. Tony knew exactly how to rile him.

"I've changed my mind!" shouted Danny. "We'll be there."

Tony turned round. "That's the right decision," he said with a patronizing smile. "See you Monday, one p.m." He started whistling to himself and strolled back up the road.

"That was Mike Butler's son, wasn't it?" asked Dad, coming out of the house with Katie trotting behind him. "What did he want?"

"Nothing," replied Danny, realizing his fists were tightly clenched.

"Didn't look like nothing."

Danny shot Dad a look. Dad shrugged his shoulders and reached into his pocket for the Mondeo's keys.

"You've done a great job," he said gratefully, admiring

the spotless car. "Thanks."

"Are *you* coming bowling, Danny?" asked Katie with hopeful eyes. She was all toothy grin, pigtails and denim dungarees.

"Not today," replied Danny.

"Oh pleeeaaaseeee!" she begged. "It's much better when you're there."

"I can't," said Danny. "I've got to speak to Carl." He had to tell Carl about Tony and the basketball match ASAP.

"Can we look at the Mondeo engine again before we go?" asked Katie.

Dad's car obsession had rubbed off on Katie too. She was usually covered in grease, spanner in hand, following Dad or Danny around and peppering them with questions.

"No, Katie," said Dad, opening the Mondeo's back door and ushering her inside. "The engine is fine. And anyway, we agreed to go bowling. Danny's got things to do and Mum's got some work to finish." Julie Sharp did the bookkeeping for a small firm of accountants.

"You'll come with us another time, won't you?" asked Katie.

"Sure," Danny nodded, giving her a smile, "just not today."

His father got in and gunned the engine.

9

Danny watched the Mondeo as it drove out of the close and then stood rooted to the spot for a few moments. He was angry with himself for caving in to Tony's taunts and accepting the basketball challenge. Yes, he and Carl could handle themselves on a basketball court, and under normal circumstances they'd stand a decent chance of winning. But the usual rules of sport didn't seem to apply when Tony Butler was playing.

In spite of the warmth of the afternoon, Danny shivered, and headed back inside.

Danny tried Carl's mobile for the next half an hour but kept getting voicemail, so after a short bus ride he found himself walking down a long dusty track past a fading black sign proclaiming SPARKS CROSS KARTING CLUB. Through his father, Danny was fascinated in cars. But he was *obsessed* with *karting* – not the little fun rides at fairgrounds, or the all year round leisure facilities. No, for Danny, karting meant the real thing.

His dad had driven karts when he was a kid but had never been that serious about it and had chucked it in aged twelve to concentrate on playing football – he'd been a decent amateur. But he thought Danny might like the sport, so just after Danny's seventh birthday Dad joined him up at Sparks Cross. Dad knew the guy who ran the place, a man called Alfie Price; they'd raced karts together when they were at primary school. From

Danny's very first lap, Alfie could see he had real potential. Danny had a natural "feel" for the sport; he handled the kart like he'd been driving for years. Plus, his attitude was spot on. Alfie could see the lad was serious about karting.

As for Danny, the minute he sat behind the wheel he was hooked. To drive a powerful kart round a track at great speed was the most incredible thrill; it made him feel like some kind of superhero in their out-of-this-world speed machine. And it wasn't just the driving he loved. He enjoyed learning about the technical aspects of the sport. He read karting magazines to check out the latest protective gear and he revelled in the camaraderie between drivers.

The racetrack at Sparks Cross looked like a slightly off-kilter figure of eight. At 1,100 metres long, it had four straights and six bends. On the site there was a clubhouse containing Alfie's office, which doubled as a signing-in room for drivers, a small meeting room/lounge, and a tiny kiosk that opened on practice days and race days. Practice days were Saturdays; race days were Sundays.

The grounds also housed a large metallic shed where the club's karts were stored. These vehicles were hired by club members who didn't own their own karts and by people – adults and children – who came on the monthly "public" days – to get a taste of what the sport was like.

The buildings at Sparks Cross were a bit shabby and in need of repair but Alfie Price refused to hike up the membership prices to pay for any upgrades.

"I want karting to be open to as many people as possible, regardless of how much money they have" was Alfie's mantra.

Danny was very conscious of the fact that lots of the world's greatest Formula One drivers had started their careers in karts: Ayrton Senna, Michael Schumacher and Alain Prost, to name but a few. He also knew that plenty of current Formula One drivers still drove karts to keep themselves fit and race-ready in between Grand Prix events. Danny was determined to rise up like them, through the karting ranks and Formula Three, into the big time. For him, Sparks Cross represented the first step on a dream path of becoming a Formula One champion.

As Danny walked round the side of the track, Alfie emerged from his office. He was just over six feet tall, with short silver hair, royal blue eyes and an L-shaped scar on his left cheek. He was wearing jeans covered in paint stains, a white T-shirt and a baseball cap.

"Danny Sharp!" grinned Alfie, walking over and giving Danny a firm handshake. He always greeted Danny like a long-lost friend, even though Danny was there every chance he got.

Alfie didn't just run Sparks Cross; he was Danny's

karting mentor, the guy Danny looked to for advice and support. And unlike Danny's dad, Alfie had stuck with the sport right through his teens. He'd been teetering on the brink of Formula One aged twenty, when he'd been involved in a terrible accident, suffering a career-ending injury to his right leg; he still walked with a limp. But he didn't seem bitter about it. In fact, Alfie was always positive, always encouraging. He was also incredibly well-connected in the Formula One world and sometimes it seemed to Danny that Alfie literally knew *everyone*.

"Here for quarter-final practice?" asked Alfie.

In just over a week Danny would be driving in the most important race of his life: the regional quarter-final heat of the National Granger Cup. This was open to all drivers in the Junior Max category – the category Danny raced in. This was a category for thirteen-to-sixteen-year-olds, so Danny often found himself racing against far older drivers. He'd done his time in the Cadet categories and had been more than ready for Junior Max when he stepped up to it, a year ago.

The vast majority of karting competitions ran like a Formula One series – you competed in a number of races per year and accrued points relating to the position in which you finished each race. At the end of the season all the points were added up and a winner emerged.

But the Granger Cup was a knockout competition and

14

Danny had made it through the first two rounds to the regional quarters. Only the first three drivers in this twelve-kart race would qualify for the semis, and those were taking place at Hardy Bridge – a very large and long-established club – in less than a month. If you made it through the semis, then you bagged a place in the final, which was going to be staged at the brand new state-of-the-art national circuit – Amber Field. Whenever he thought about the upcoming quarter-final, Danny's stomach went into crazed gymnastic mode. He was nervous and scared and excited all at the same time. And the event was bearing down on him like an out-of-control monster truck.

Danny shook his head. "I'm here for a paint job," he told Alfie.

"Sounds reasonable. Got everything you need?"

Danny nodded.

"Any progress on sponsorship?" asked Alfie. "We need some financial clout behind you."

If you wanted to progress right up through the karting ranks and make it into Formula Three and beyond, you needed money behind you; the kind of money that only a sponsor – like a big company – could bring. They'd back you financially and in return their "brand" would be connected with a (hopefully) top driver.

"Dad says he wants to wait for the right moment to

approach people," replied Danny. "He wants to hit sponsors at the 'optimum' time. I want to approach people now."

"Your dad knows what he's doing," replied Alfie. "I'm sure he'll get on the case very soon."

Danny shrugged his shoulders.

"Anyway," said Alfie, "I've got some calls to make. Have a crack at your kart and make sure you look in on me before you go."

With that, Alfie headed back into his office and Danny walked over to the kart shed. He slid open its huge metal doors and stepped inside, the smell of engine oil and metallic paint instantly hitting him. He flicked a switch and bright lights suddenly illuminated the space. All of the club's karts sat in a neat row, silent and still, like battle robots waiting for their launch command. He walked down the row and stopped at the end. There, right in front of him, was his own kart. After years of racing the club's vehicles, Danny still couldn't quite believe that he had his own machine.

It had been a surprise Christmas present.

He'd never forget the moment Dad had called him outside on Christmas Eve, saying he needed some help putting up some more outdoor lights. As Danny stepped out, there it was – in the middle of their small back garden – gleaming in the moonlight. It looked incredible, with orange and yellow waves on the side pods and deep red arrows on the nose cone and rear bar.

"*No way!*" whispered Danny, his heart seeming to stop.

"I couldn't wait till tomorrow," Dad said before Danny started going crazy, jumping in the air, running round the yard and hugging Dad repeatedly, as Mum and Katie came out to see what all of the fuss was about. Mum knew about the present. She worried a lot about Danny's safety when he was behind the wheel of a kart, and for this reason she'd never seen him drive, not even when he was practising. She'd kept Katie away too – in case Danny crashed and it was a gruesome spectacle. But she knew how much the sport meant to him, and had scrimped and saved with Dad to make the kart purchase possible.

Katie felt terribly jealous when she first set eyes on the kart. But when Dad brought out a massive toy garage for her, complete with raised work ramps and tyre inflators, she raced inside to get all of her toy cars and start playing with it.

It had taken Danny quite a while to calm down after his initial euphoria on seeing the kart, but when he stopped his leaping, he crouched down to examine it at close quarters.

"It's got a 125cc two-stroke water-cooled engine,"

said Dad. "And it's TAG – Touch and Go – which gives you a motorized standing start. Plus it does zero to sixty in three and a half seconds."

Danny stared in awe at the motor machine, its steel tube chassis and alloy wheels giving it a sparkling, futuristic look. It was hard to believe it was actually his!

"It's only three years old," added Dad. "I got it off Spike."

Spike Thomas was an old friend of Dad's who ran a kart repair shop called The Kart Kit. Spike had raced karts with Alfie and Dad when they were kids.

"It's been in a couple of accidents," Dad continued, "but Spike's spent a lot of time on it. He says it's in excellent shape."

Danny smiled as he remembered that night and walked over to a wooden workbench. He prised open a pot of metallic red paint with a screwdriver, and then carried the pot and a specialized brush back to his kart. It was fitted with "slicks" – slick tyres – at the minute, because they best suited the current dry weather. At full speed it could do seventy mph, which Danny found incredible. Seventy was the national speed limit, the fastest any adult was allowed to drive, on a motorway or major A road. Yet when he was out there on the track he could go just as fast – it was incredible!

Some of the paint on the left side of his kart had

peeled away, so Danny spent an hour peeling the remaining flakes away and smoothing the affected area with very strong sandpaper. He then very carefully repainted the blank patch until he was fully satisfied. He was just standing back to admire his work when his mobile bleeped. His phone was his dad's old and battered one, but it did the job.

CARL read the display.

This was good. Danny needed to tell Carl about the basketball game. He'd meant to ring him again, but had got distracted by working on his kart. But before he could say anything, Carl's voice exploded on the line.

"Listen up, Danny," said his best mate with great excitement. "I've got some *brilliant* news!"

After finishing the paint job, saying goodbye to Alfie and getting the bus home, Danny ran down Grassmere Close, just in time to see a bearded man with straggly hair driving away in the gleaming Mondeo. Dad had got his sale. He was holding a large wad of notes and looked very pleased with himself.

"You're not going to believe this," panted Danny, "but you know that massive exhibition day at the F-NEX Arena tomorrow?"

Dad nodded.

"Well, Carl's mum just got given three tickets; one for Carl, one for me and one for you!"

Carl's mum worked for an events company and was always getting freebies.

"They'll be racing loads of cars and motorbikes and demonstrating some new Formula One designs," Danny went on. "But the best bit is that Scot Devlin's going to race his Malloy Formula One car against two BMW street cars. It's going to be crazy!"

Malloy were the manufacturing team that Scot Devlin drove for. They'd never had a champion. Devlin was their big hope. He'd only been racing Formula One for a couple of years, but he was already in fifth position on this season's leader board – not bad for a rookie. He also happened to be Danny's Formula One hero.

"Don't you think that's just showboating?" asked Dad, who could be a bit of a Formula One snob.

"No way!" replied Danny. "David Coulthard raced street cars, didn't he?"

"Fair point," nodded Dad. "You're on!"

"Yessss!" cried Danny, clenching his fist in celebration.

Danny went to his room, fizzing with excitement. He lay down on his bed, folded his arms behind his head and gazed up at the posters that fought for space on his walls; alongside the pictures of Lewis Hamilton, Ayrton Senna and Michael Schumacher were shots of Devlin. Danny couldn't believe he was going to be seeing a real Formula One star race tomorrow. Talk about a great start to the summer holidays!

"Danny! Come and lay the table!" shouted his mum from the kitchen.

Danny snapped out of his reverie, dragged himself off

his bed and headed downstairs. He glanced out of the window next to the front door and saw Dad on the pavement, his brow furrowed as he read a letter. Danny opened the front door. The second Dad spotted Danny, he quickly stuffed the letter into his trouser pocket.

"What's that?" asked Danny with interest.

"It's, er . . . it's a bill," replied Dad. "They just keep on coming!"

Danny gave him a funny look. It wasn't like Dad to be secretive, especially about something as boring as a bill. But he'd whipped it out of sight pretty sharpish when Danny opened the door. As Danny walked into the kitchen and started setting the table, he felt pretty sure about one thing. That letter wasn't a bill. For some strange reason, Dad had been lying.

4

"Danny, Carl's here!" called Mum at nine-fifteen the following morning.

Danny sat up in bed and rubbed his eyes. What was he doing today? And then it hit him. The F-NEX Arena; seeing Scot Devlin race street cars! Danny leapt out of bed, pulled on his clothes and raced downstairs, swerving round the corner into the kitchen.

"Slow down!" laughed Carl. "I'm your manager and I need you in one piece!"

Carl was wearing tracksuit trousers, an oversized green T-shirt and battered black trainers.

"When did you get here?" asked Danny, pouring some cornflakes into a bowl and drenching them in milk.

"Two minutes ago," replied Carl.

"Have you had breakfast, Carl?" asked Mum, as Danny tucked in.

"Yes, thanks," said Carl.

"Where's Dad?" asked Danny.

"He's just putting some stuff in the van."

Dad was famous for his trip preparations. From a cinema visit to a two-week summer holiday, he always took stacks of food and drink. "There's no way I'm going to pay those rip-off prices" was his comment about the goods available at sporting or leisure venues. Danny knew he was right but if it was up to him he'd just buy stuff at the F-NEX Arena. It might be more expensive but it would be so much easier!

Katie ran into the kitchen holding her motorbike rucksack.

"Are you driving in a race today, Danny?" she asked, gazing up at him.

He laughed and ruffled her hair. "Not today. We're going to watch some other people racing."

"Right, young man," said Mum, facing Danny. "I'm taking Katie to play at Angela's house, so I'll say goodbye now. Be good, both of you, and listen to Dad."

"Yes, Mum," groaned Danny with embarrassment.

Mum squeezed his shoulder and then bustled Katie outside.

Ten minutes later, Dad pulled his van – a second-hand maroon Fiat Doblò, with plenty of storage space for car parts – out of the close, Danny and Carl sitting up front with him. Dad flicked on a radio station playing "golden oldies", and started humming along with the tune.

"How can you listen to this rubbish?" demanded Danny, flicking it to another station pumping out heavy beats.

"Now that really *is* rubbish!" said Dad, trying to switch the station back. He and Danny fought over the controls.

"Hey!" shouted Carl, worried this mini feud might cause an accident. He turned off the radio. Danny and Dad looked at him and both started laughing.

"OK," said Dad, "no music."

As they left the asphalt and tightly packed buildings of the city and began driving through open countryside, they started playing "Spot the Flashest Car". The nearer they got to the venue, the flasher the cars got. Carl spotted a Red Porsche 911 GT3, and Danny rivalled it with a silver Lamborghini LP460.

"Those are the kind of cars we'll be driving one day," laughed Carl.

An hour later the van reached the brow of a hill and the F-NEX Arena came into view. Instead of plonking the venue in the heart of the city, the owners had opted for an out-of-town location with excellent road and rail links, so it stood with green land all around it. None of them had been there before and they all gasped at the sheer size of the place. It was absolutely massive – the size of a

South American football stadium. Thousands of mirrored panels on the building's exterior shimmered in the sunshine. A gigantic silver sign declaring "F-NEX ARENA" hung proudly on the front of the venue.

All around them hundreds of vehicles were parking in the vast banks of car parks and thousands of spectators were migrating towards the venue on foot.

"Excellent!" mouthed Carl.

Dad pulled the van into a space and the three of them piled out. "This way," he announced and they joined the massive throng of people. When they approached the building, they saw hundreds of stewards in fluorescent orange jackets – stationed by the turnstiles, checking tickets, searching bags and ushering people through. Carl produced the tickets and after a short queue they were in.

Everything about the inside of the building was huge: the wall-mounted plasma screens showing Formula One highlights, the merchandizing areas with T-shirts, hoodies and DVDs, and the food kiosks serving outrageously big tubs of popcorn. Danny gazed longingly at the sizzling pizza slices and jumbo burgers that were being served.

"Forget about it," said Dad, following Danny's hungry gaze and pointing at the food-stacked rucksack on his back.

Carl's mum had been given excellent tickets: lower tier,

just five rows back and right near the middle. A huge oval track had been laid down round the edge of the arena with powerful floodlights illuminating the space. The massively high grey roof seemed to be several light years above them.

The seats filled up quickly and in no time at all, the event kicked off. First up were some motorbike riders who performed huge leaps over an ever-lengthening row of cars and then did some mind-boggling, mid-air bike changes. Danny and Carl cheered and screamed with the rest of the crowd. Then came a team of professional stunt drivers who performed death-defying near-crashes, side drives and escapes from burning vehicles.

"AWESOME!" shouted Danny. Dad was caught up in the excitement and was cheering too.

After this were some stock car smash-ups, quad bike obstacle races and motorbike team formations – the best one had fifteen people on one bike! Then there was then a lull in the proceedings, during which Dad handed out some grub – sandwiches, crisps, apples and Coke. The boys wolfed it all down.

"AND NOW, LADIES AND GENTLEMEN," roared the announcer, "FOR OUR SHOWPIECE EVENT, I GIVE YOU THE BMW CHALLENGERS!"

"This is it!" hissed Danny, nudging Carl in the ribs.

Two BMW X6Ms appeared on the track, one blue, one

red, their windows tinted, their chrome wheels glittering in the spotlight.

"Outrageous!" mouthed Carl.

"BOTH OF THESE TOP-OF-THE-RANGE VEHICLES FEATURE BMW'S UNIQUE FOUR-WHEEL-DRIVE SYSTEM WITH DYNAMIC PERFORMANCE CONTROL!" boomed the announcer. "AND WITH TOP SPEEDS OF ONE HUNDRED AND SEVENTY MILES PER HOUR, THESE ARE SERIOUSLY FAST CARS!"

The crowd screamed with excitement.

"AND NOW, THE MAN CHALLENGING THEM OVER A TEN LAP, TEN-THOUSAND-METRE COURSE. . ."

"It's him!" shouted Danny.

". . .CURRENTLY FIFTH ON THE FORMULA ONE SERIES LEADER BOARD . . . THE DRIVER EVERYONE IS TALKING ABOUT . . . MR SCOT DEVLIN!"

Danny, Carl and Dad leapt to their feet.

"There he is!" shouted Danny.

Striding across the track, in a purple and black suit – with his team's name, MALLOY, stretched across his chest – was Scot Devlin. Tall, with ash-blond hair and piercing blue eyes, Devlin carried his helmet with one hand and waved to the ecstatic crowd with the other.

And then about twenty metres behind him, from a side opening, appeared a team of six techies, pushing one of Devlin's Malloy Formula One cars. They stopped when they reached a thick white line painted on the track, fifty metres or so from the starting/finishing line.

Danny gaped at the vehicle. He'd been to several Grand Prix races before but he'd never been anything like this close. If he sprang out of his seat he would almost be able to land in the vehicle and take it for a test drive.

It was a glorious machine with a sleek black body bearing the letters NEW-CALL – Team Malloy's sponsors – in bright purple, down its centre, on each front wing and on its rear bar. Danny could see the web of black metal struts connecting the wheels to the car, the two black seat belt straps, the curved metal dome above the driver's seat, and the widening chassis behind the driver's seat that contained the engine and narrowed to a point on the rear wing.

"Eighteen-thousand revs," Danny shouted at Carl above the crowd. "Top speed – two hundred and forty mph, and it's got an energy-recovering system that gives Devlin up to six seconds boost per lap. It's the business – the dream car!"

"Brilliant!" yelled Carl.

"AND NOW FOR THE CHALLENGE!" cried the announcer. "ALL THREE CARS MUST COMPLETE TEN LAPS, BUT THE BMWS WILL HAVE A TWO-LAP HEAD START ON THEIR FORMULA ONE OPPONENT. WE HAVE TAKEN INTO ACCOUNT ALL THE RELEVANT SPEED AND

TURBULENCE FACTORS AND THIS WILL MAKE IT A LEVEL RACE. IS EVERYONE IN THE ARENA READY FOR THIS?"

The crowd went wild, their noise rising to a near-deafening crescendo.

"DRIVERS, TAKE YOUR POSITIONS!"

The BMWs drove towards the starting line. Scot Devlin gave the crowd one more wave, had a quick conversation with his team and then lowered himself into the cockpit of his car. He affixed the seat belts, gripped the wheel and nodded.

A man with a green flag appeared at the side of the track and positioned himself so that all three drivers could see him. He then raised his flag high into the air. The tension in the arena was so intense that Danny felt as if the air was being strangled out of him. For a few seconds nothing happened.

Then the man brought down his flag.

There was a colossal roar as the two BMW engines revved into action; they were off!

Danny's eyes stretched in awe as the X6Ms broke from the starting line, accelerating furiously.

"Four point seven seconds to sixty mph!" he shouted excitedly. The BMWs shot down the straight, side by side. They took the first corner in unison, reminding Danny of synchronized swimmers. After a precise and fast lap, they sped down the home straight and across the finish line.

Devlin's car was roaring at the side, like a snorting beast waiting to ensnare its prey.

On cruised the BMWs into their second lap.

"How's he ever going to catch them?" shouted Carl as the Beamers sped round the track again.

"Just watch him!" yelled Danny, pointing to the track, where the ferocious roar of Devlin's engine was pumping noisily into the arena. The X6Ms powered towards the finish line for a second time.

This was Devlin's cue and just as they reached him, he launched into the race.

"GO FOR IT!" screamed Danny.

Devlin accelerated ferociously but the BMWs were already driving at full speed, so he had a lot to do. His car pummelled the track, taking his first – and the street cars' third – lap in a flash of noise and colour. The three cars were side by side. It was a breathtaking scene – to see Devlin driving with such grace and power. By their fourth lap Devlin was pushing his car just above two hundred mph. On lap five, he overtook the BMWs on the home straight in a dashing manoeuvre. This was excellent, but it still left him just under two laps behind them.

On their sixth and his fourth lap, Devlin pushed ahead, and at the end of their seventh lap, he had caught up a whole lap. He was now just one lap behind them. The BMWs didn't let up and halfway through their eighth lap

Devlin was still three quarters of a lap behind them. They seemed completely determined to crush his race prospects. On lap nine though, his car seemed to go into overdrive. With an expert match of precision steering and acceleration he closed the gap further, taking the final bend in majestic style.

"Did you see how he took that corner!" shouted Dad. "That was top class!"

As the X6Ms hit the finish line of lap nine, Devlin still trailed them by a hundred metres. If he could overtake them on their tenth and final lap, he would be the winner.

And he was giving it everything.

By the time the three cars took the final bend of lap ten, Devlin was only twenty-five metres behind the BMWs. But the street cars suddenly closed ranks, swerving towards each other to form a speeding metallic barrier. There seemed to be no way through.

But Devlin had other plans.

With the final finish line in sight, his car exploded with a terrifying burst of speed. The BMWs had no choice but to part. The gap was small, but just big enough for Devlin to shoot through and avoid scratching their sides by millimetres.

"YESSS!" yelled Danny, leaping up and down as Devlin careered across the finish line, a metre in front of the BMWs.

"INCREDIBLE!" shouted Carl, astounded by the skill and sheer force of Devlin's driving.

"That was something else," said Dad, as they left their seats and walked with the crowds in the direction of the exits. "I was wrong about it just being showboating. Devlin had to use all of his wits and skill to beat them – it was an excellent performance; well worth seeing."

Everyone around them was buzzing – like they'd all just driven in the race themselves. The arena's food outlets and merchandise stalls were doing a roaring trade.

"Can we hang around a bit?" asked Danny as they walked out of the arena into bright sunshine.

"What for?" asked Dad.

"I want to get Devlin's autograph."

"Me too!" nodded Carl. "When Danny's a top Formula One driver everyone will want *his* autograph. And as his manager, some people will definitely want *mine*!"

Danny laughed.

"OK," smiled Dad. "But we're only waiting half an hour. I don't want to spend all day here."

Danny and Carl were already gone, racing round the outside of the arena, searching for the stage door. They finally located it by spotting the two burly security guards standing outside, their arms folded, their eyes scanning the already sizable crowd that had gathered in front of some crash barriers.

Everyone was talking about Devlin's performance; lots of people were saying he had a real chance to become Formula One champion, if not this year, then next.

A few minutes later Danny spotted a short greasy-haired guy with a shiny grey suit and grey tie weaving his way through the crowd and past the barriers. One of the guards stepped over to him and they held a brief conversation.

"Look who it is," muttered Dad.

"Who?" asked Danny.

"He's called Vince Dutton," replied Dad. "He calls himself a journalist but real journalists are supposed to be impartial – report on the facts, tell the truth. That guy has a deal with Verdant."

The Verdant and Malloy Formula One manufacturing teams were arch rivals.

"Dutton is always looking for dirt on Malloy and its drivers," explained Dad. "He's known as 'The Attack Dog' – he'll bite people's heads off if he's paid enough. He's a nasty piece of work – the sort of person you'd do well to avoid in life."

Danny watched as Dutton finished his conversation with the guard and handed him something. The guard nodded and indicated that Dutton could remain there, closest to the stage door.

Dad checked his watch. "OK, boys, half an hour's up. Let's go."

But at that moment there were cries from the front of the mass. The stage door was opening. A tall woman with long blonde hair came out in a spangly silver dress, closely followed by Devlin, who was wearing huge sunglasses and a designer hoodie. There were shouts and screams from the crowd. People surged forward, lots of them holding out photos of Devlin for him to sign.

But before he could talk to anyone, Vince Dutton collared him. He obviously said something that didn't please the Formula One star, because Devlin leant forward, hissed some words back into Dutton's ears and then started hurrying off, away from the stadium.

The crowd were so shocked that they took a few moments to respond. As people surged forward, Devlin and the woman ducked into a waiting people carrier and the vehicle swiftly pulled away. There were groans from the disappointed crowd, and nobody groaned louder than Danny Sharp. "I can't believe he just ran off like that without doing autographs!" he complained bitterly.

Danny and Carl were quiet on the journey home. Some of the excitement and enthusiasm generated by the race had been punctured by Devlin's sharp exit.

"That's the way some of these modern celebrities behave," Dad told them. "In my day, it was a point of principle to stay behind, meet the fans and sign as many autographs as you could. None of this running away at the first sign of trouble – however unpleasant Vince Dutton can be."

When they got home, Dad went off to phone someone about a Peugeot estate car he'd been checking out. Danny and Carl got some drinks and crisps and went out to sit in the garden.

"Are you around on Monday afternoon at about one?" asked Danny casually.

"Yeah," replied Carl, "why? What's happening?"

"Er . . . you and me are playing Tony Butler and Kev Rowntree in a two v two basketball match. Losers pay winners twenty quid," replied Danny breezily, as if this were an everyday sort of arrangement.

Carl nearly choked on his mouthful of crisps. "You're joking, right?"

Danny shook his head.

"Are you crazy?" said Carl. "Kev is like the Incredible Hulk but with less brains. And Tony's never observed a rule of any sport in his life. Remember how he busted Nigel Williams's hand? We'll be mincemeat!"

"No, we won't," insisted Danny. "We're easily good enough to beat them!"

"But what if we lose?" said Carl. "We'll have to pay them twenty pounds!"

"Chill out," replied Danny, "we won't lose."

But despite being upbeat with Carl, Danny was really beginning to regret accepting Tony's challenge. Yes, he and Carl were better players than Tony and Kev, but Tony never played fair. Why hadn't Danny just stuck to his guns and said no? Being called "chicken" wasn't the end of the world. He went inside to get more drinks. Maybe Carl was right; come Monday, they might well be mincemeat.

5

"I've been thinking about how to get you in the best shape for the Granger Cup quarter-final," said Alfie Price, "and I think we need to focus on your overtaking."

Alfie made a cup of tea for himself and poured a glass of apple juice for Danny. It was Sunday morning and they were sitting in the office at Sparks Cross.

"I've told you a million times but you still haven't quite got it when it comes to the overtake," went on Alfie. "Don't look at the car in front of you, look at the gap. You're not going to drive through the *car,* you're going to drive through the *gap.* You've got to work on that aspect of your driving if you want to make the semis."

"I know," replied Danny, while bristling a little at the criticism. "But when you're out there your instinct is to watch where everyone else is."

"Of course that's what your instinct tells you," agreed

Alfie, "and of course you need to be aware of where the other karts are. But you've got to be thinking of your entrance and exit for the next corner – you've got to be one step ahead of everyone else. Sometimes you're not doing that."

Danny knew that Alfie was right; he usually was when it came to karting matters.

"Look," went on Alfie, "some people say racing is just about ECT – engine, chassis and tyres. They reckon you could put a robot in there and they'd do the job as well as a human. But that's rubbish. The driver is the crucible – the centre of the whole enterprise – and skilful overtaking can shave seconds off your time. I want to show you something."

He reached for a disc, stuck it in the office DVD player and flicked on the old-fashioned TV. The screen burst into life. The word OVERTAKING zipped across the top of the screen, and what followed was an amazing montage of Formula One drivers overtaking other cars at tracks all round the world, from Monaco to Indianapolis. There was Button, Alonso, Schumacher, Hamilton and Barrichello, each with their own style, but each firmly in control of their vehicle; driving through the gaps and making it past the opposition, on the inside, on the outside, through the middle.

The DVD lasted about twenty minutes and by the end

of it Danny was re-energized. Alfie's pep talks and pointers always seemed to have that effect on him.

Danny was in an excellent mood by the time he got home. He was just about to go upstairs to get changed when Mum appeared at the kitchen doorway.

"Hey, Danny," she smiled, "could you come in here for a moment?"

Danny eyed her suspiciously. Her tone sounded formal and that was unusual. Hesitantly he stepped into the kitchen. She shut the door behind him and they sat down at the table.

"What's up?" he asked.

"There are some new timetables being introduced at Dad's work," she said. "He might lose a shift or two."

"Really?" asked Danny, surprised.

"Don't worry," said Mum brightly, "it's no big deal — it's happening throughout the postal service. If it does happen, I'll just take on some more bookkeeping jobs."

Danny felt a pang of anxiety in his chest. "Have we got money problems?" he asked.

"Money's always a little bit tight, you know that," replied Mum. "But we should be fine if I take on some extra work."

Danny frowned. Mum worked pretty hard already. And then a twinge of disappointment hit him. He knew it was selfish, but he badly needed some new karting gloves. If money was scarce he'd have to forget about any karting-related purchases.

"I don't want Katie knowing anything about it," said Mum, eyeing the shut kitchen door.

"Sure," nodded Danny.

"It will mean I'll need some extra help from you," said Mum, "you know, with babysitting and stuff."

"No problem."

They were silent for a few seconds. "It's no big deal," smiled Mum, "it will only be a few extra hours a week."

"It's fine, Mum," said Danny, trying to mask his disappointment. "Just let me know when you need me."

"You're a good lad," smiled Mum, touching his shoulder.

Danny stood up and exited the kitchen. While not buying new karting gloves was a pain, there was something far more important on Danny's mind at that moment: the basketball match against Tony and Kev – tomorrow.

6

"I'm amazed you showed up!" sneered Tony Butler.

He winked at the five figures he'd brought along as spectators. They stood behind the fence of the basketball court.

"Wouldn't miss the chance to batter you!" replied Danny, far more confidently than he felt.

Danny and Carl had spent most of the previous evening practising in Danny's back garden, motivated partly by fear and partly by the fact that they didn't want to lose twenty pounds.

"Kev's big but not very fast," Danny had reminded Carl, "and Tony's a cheat. He'll foul us and say it was nothing, but if we can break clear from him, we can score – I'm telling you."

"What do you want?" demanded Tony, bending his knees to warm up. "Ends or centre?"

"Doesn't bother us," replied Danny coolly.

"Suit yourself," shrugged Tony, "you can have centre."

He aimed a fierce bounce pass straight at Danny's chest. Danny's hands shot out and caught it in mid-flight. Tony scowled.

"We'll play two halves of fifteen minutes each," declared Tony.

Danny and Carl looked at each other and nodded in agreement. Tony scampered off to have a last minute team-talk with Kev. Danny eyed Tony's co-player warily; he really was a big lad.

Ten seconds later the ball was in play. Danny and Carl had most of the early possession and when Carl's overhead pass evaded Kev, Danny sneaked in behind him and netted a basket from close range. 2–0.

Tony and Kev came back immediately, Tony going on a long mazy run before scoring from just outside the arc, giving him and Kev a 3–2 lead. Their supporters cheered them on.

Next, a long shot from Carl was blocked by Kev and on the break, Tony narrowly missed netting a basket. There were a few minutes of backwards and forwards movements, but without a basket. In the last couple of minutes of the first half, Carl scored with an athletic jump shot, but a minute later, after picking up a rebound, Kev launched himself into the air and slam-dunked the ball.

At half-time it was 5–4 to Tony and Kev.

"We're doing OK," said Danny in the break, as he and Carl had a drink at one side of the court while Tony and Kev stood on the opposite side, chatting and joking with their motley rent-a-crowd.

"You were right about Kev being slow," said Carl. "We both got past him a couple of times."

"I told you, it's their weakness," nodded Danny. "Let's exploit it more in the second half."

The second half began in a tense fashion, with both teams giving away possession several times. But then Carl released Danny with a pinpoint long pass. Danny caught the ball at chest height and thrust forward, dribbling the ball low to the ground. Tony went to grab it but Danny switched direction and Tony plunged on to the ground. Kev advanced menacingly forward. Danny dragged the ball round him and was about to move on when Tony stuck out a leg and tripped him.

"FOUL!" yelled Danny and Carl at the same time.

"NO WAY!" shouted Tony.

Kev glanced at Tony – a look that reluctantly said, *Give it to them.*

Tony scowled and shrugged his shoulders. "OK," he said bitterly.

Danny hurried over to the foul line and held the ball at the top of his chest before launching his attempt. The ball arced through the air, hit the backboard and dipped into the baskets: 5–5.

"BRILLIANT!" grinned Carl, running up to Danny and exchanging a high five. But to Danny's disappointment, he missed with his second foul shot.

Following this, Tony and Danny both netted long shots to make it 8–8, and then Carl had a very near miss from long distance. Danny checked his watch. There were only two minutes left to play. If he and Carl could hang on, their reputations and their twenty pounds would be safe.

But then Kev came thudding forward, not fast, but powerfully dribbling the ball, left and right. Danny tried to steal the ball, but Kev spun round and avoided him. Kev made as if he were going to pass to Tony, so Carl jumped in this path, but it was a dummy, giving Kev just enough time to leap into the air and net with a high jump shot.

10–8 to the opposition with less than a minute left; disaster! Danny could taste the bitter flavour of defeat. But he wasn't going to give up. So when Carl released him with a pass, he gritted his teeth and went on a swerving run, feinting passes, dribbling at speed, and evading challenges from both Tony and Kev. As the seconds dripped away, he reached the opposition basket and leapt as high as he could. Reaching the peak of his jump he released the ball.

It hit the backboard and bounced down against the rim of the basket. For an agonizing second it looked as if it would bounce away from the basket, but it shot straight into the net.

"INCREDIBLE!" yelled Carl, running over to congratulate Danny. It felt like they'd just won the World Cup. Danny checked his watch. Time was up.

"That basket doesn't count," snapped Tony sourly.

"What?" demanded Danny, his elation evaporating instantly.

"You *carried* the ball," glared Tony.

"No he didn't!" hit back Carl. "It was a fair basket!"

"We win ten to eight," insisted Tony. "You owe us twenty pounds."

A taut wire inside Danny snapped and suddenly he was in Tony's face, squaring up to him. "In your dreams, CHEATER!" he yelled.

"You want some?" yelled Tony, his eyes bulging with rage.

"LEAVE IT, DANNY!" shouted Carl, pulling his friend away. Luckily, Kev performed the same move on Tony and the two would-be combatants were separated like snarling warriors.

"The basket was good and you know it!" yelled Danny. "You just can't take it that we drew with you! You're a cheat!"

"And you're a liar!" screamed Tony, but Kev was bustling him away to the other side of the court. Tony tried to break free but Kev's grip held.

Tony shook his fist at Danny. "I haven't finished with you yet, Sharp!" He spat the words out.

"Yeah, yeah!" called back Danny. "I'm trembling in my trainers!"

"Come on," said Carl, leading Danny away, "let's go."

As they walked home, part of Danny was proud that he'd stood up to Tony, but another part was annoyed with himself for losing it and getting physical. Tony had said he hadn't finished with him yet. What did he mean by that? Back at his house Danny tried to put all thoughts of Tony Butler out of his mind, but it was hard – very hard.

Carl stayed at Danny's for what was left of the afternoon, but then his mum phoned and said he had to come home for supper. Danny got in an hour on *Power Wheels 7*, but Anton Le Grand was in no mood for compromise, so Danny's attempts to jump ahead of him on the leader board failed miserably.

After his virtual efforts he wandered down to the kitchen. Katie was sitting at the table concentrating on a drawing. She looked up when Danny came in and jumped off her chair to give him a bone-crushing hug. "Danny, do you want to see my picture?" she said. This was more of a command than a question.

"Of course," said Danny.

She led him to the table and showed him her artwork. It was of a light blue sports car with rear spoiler and alloy wheels. She'd put in the wheel spokes and hubcaps.

Katie had a good eye for detail.

"Do you like it?" she asked.

"It's brilliant!" grinned Danny, ruffling her hair.

"Do you think when Dad lets me start racing karts, I'll be as good as you?" she asked with big, expectant eyes.

"Of course you will!" replied Danny. "You'll probably be better!"

"Do you really think so?"

"Sure," grinned Danny.

Dad had promised Katie she could join Sparks Cross and start karting next year when she was seven – the same age Danny had been when he started. Mum was worried about this, but she had decided to be fair. If Danny began karting when he was seven, then Katie could too. But having heard what Mum had said about money being tight, Danny reckoned it would probably be a very long time before Katie got her own kart, if ever. She'd have to use the club's machines.

"I've already seen the helmet I want to get when I start karting," Katie told him. "It was in one of your magazines. It's red with white stripes. It looks brilliant!"

"You go for it," nodded Danny, not wanting to spoil her dreams with a harsh dose of financial reality.

"I'm just going to get some more colours," chirped Katie, running out of the kitchen.

Danny sat down at the table. There was a pile of letters

in the middle and he started flicking through them. He'd only reached the third one when suddenly the whole stack was whisked out of his hands.

It was Dad.

He held the letters firmly in his hand.

"What's going on?" demanded Danny.

"Nothing," replied Dad, looking shifty. "I just need to go through some of these. Bills and more bills."

"I've never seen you so eager to pay bills," remarked Danny suspiciously.

"New regime," said Dad quickly. "I want to pay things on the day they come in instead of letting them pile up – you know, be more efficient."

Danny gave him a funny look. He remembered how Dad had hurriedly tucked another letter out of sight the other day.

"Anyway, Mum said supper's in five minutes," said Dad, quickly changing the subject.

And with that, he walked out of the kitchen. Danny sat at the table trying to figure out what was going on.

And that's when it hit him.

What had Mum told him?

There are some new timetables being introduced at Dad's work. He might lose a shift or two.

An icy shiver curled down his spine. The letters must be connected to Dad's job. That's why Dad had been so shifty with them. The situation must be far worse than Mum had said. Forget Dad losing a couple of shifts, the post office must be making him *redundant*! Danny had heard about post office redundancies a while back but he'd reckoned it had nothing to do with him or his family. Well, forget buying new karting gloves; Dad losing his job would be a complete disaster. They'd have to sell the house and move somewhere smaller – if they could afford it. No wonder Mum hadn't wanted Katie to hear anything. But why hadn't his parents told him the whole truth?

At supper, Danny had no appetite.

"Are you all right?" asked Mum as she took away his mostly unfinished supper.

"Yeah," he nodded, "I'm just tired."

His parents exchanged a quick glance.

"Will you play car racing with me?" asked Katie, approaching his chair and tugging his elbow.

"Not tonight," cut in Mum. "It's bath and bed for you, young lady."

"Oh, Mum!" cried Katie.

"No, Katie," said Mum firmly.

After clearing the table, Danny and Dad did the washing-up. Dad gave him several sideways looks to see how he was doing, but Danny ignored them. Danny's obstinate streak had made him decide that if his parents weren't going to tell him the truth about Dad's work situation, then he wouldn't ask them; he'd just find out for himself.

After the kitchen was back in order, Danny went to his room and lay on his bed, listening to a football match on the radio. In the half-time break, his mobile went. He expected it to be Carl, but the name flashing was ALFIE.

Alfie didn't usually call him at night.

"Hey, Alfie, is everything OK?"

"Everything's better than OK," replied Alfie.

"How?" asked Danny.

"I have some excellent news."

Danny sat up. "What sort of news is it?" he asked excitedly.

"I've just organized some work experience for you."

"What?" asked Danny, confused. Wasn't work experience for older kids? "Where is it?" he enquired.

"At the Malloy team's Formula One headquarters!"

"No way!" cried Danny, his head almost exploding with delight and shock.

"Totally!" laughed Alfie. "Bill Moore in the marketing department is an old mate of mine and he's arranged it. I thought it would do you good to get a bit closer to the sport – you know, see behind the scenes. He's sorted out four days for you there."

Danny's body was fizzing with excitement. "This is

incredible, Alfie! You're a genius! Thank you, thank you!"

"It's a pleasure," laughed Alfie.

"When do I start?"

There was a short, dramatic pause.

"Tomorrow," replied Alfie.

Danny had gone completely crazy when he came off the phone to Alfie. He'd run around the house screaming hysterically. When he'd calmed down, he told his parents what was happening.

"You have to hand it to Alfie," smiled Dad. "The man really knows his way around Formula One! I can't imagine there will be too many kids hanging out at Malloy HQ this summer!"

"Will you see anyone famous?" asked Katie.

"Probably not," laughed Danny, "but it will be a great chance to look behind the scenes."

"I'm thrilled for you," Mum had beamed, before ushering Katie back to bed and telling Danny not to stay up half the night reading karting magazines or speaking to Carl on his mobile.

And now, just twelve hours later, Danny was sitting

beside Alfie in Alfie's battered ex-army jeep, driving up the motorway in the direction of Malloy HQ. Half an hour later, they came off the motorway, took several turnings and then drove down a road leading to a large green building, surrounded by a high fence – its roof solar panels glinting sharply in the sun. Danny had seen pictures of the building in magazines before and on telly but this was the real thing!

"OK?" asked Alfie as they pulled up in the car park.

Danny gulped nervously. Whatever he did inside the building he was desperate to make a good impression.

"Let's do it," said Alfie.

Together they strode across the asphalt, through a revolving door and into an echoey stone-floored lobby. A large curving wooden desk stood on the left, behind which sat a smartly dressed young woman with a neat bob hairstyle. Beside her was a tight-jawed security guard in a blue uniform. On the right-hand wall were several huge black and white photos of Malloy's current crop of stars; Ian Gill, Freddy Rawlings and of course, Scot Devlin.

"Good morning," said Alfie to the woman at the desk. "This is Danny Sharp. He's doing some work experience here. And I'm Alfie Price. We're here to see Bill Moore at nine-thirty."

The woman nodded and punched some numbers into

her phone. "Mr Moore," she said, "it's Roberta from reception. I have Alfie Price and Danny Sharp here."

She waited for a response and then put down the phone. "Mr Moore will be with you in a minute," she smiled. "Alberto here will give you your passes. You need to wear these at all times during your visit."

"No problem," smiled Alfie. "Thank you."

Alberto duly handed over two passes. Alfie and Danny put these on and went to sit on the sofas opposite the desk. Danny's hands felt clammy and his stomach was jangling with nerves. Alfie winked at him reassuringly. A couple of minutes later, a ruddy-faced man with thinning grey hair and a bulbous nose came out of a lift and walked towards them. Danny and Alfie both stood.

"Alfie Price!" beamed Bill, giving Alfie a fulsome handshake. "And you must be Danny," he added, crunching Danny's hand. "I hear you're an aspiring Formula One driver."

Danny blushed. "Sort of," he replied.

"Excellent!" laughed Bill, "We're always looking for new talent and this guy. . ." he put a friendly arm round Alfie's shoulder ". . .is the finest person to have as your coach."

"That's enough!" laughed Alfie, but Danny could see he liked the praise.

Bill led them into the lift and hit the button for the second floor.

"Excited about being here?" Bill smiled at Danny.

"Totally!" Danny replied. "It's . . . brilliant!"

"Good! We're delighted to have you!"

Danny's whole body shook with anticipation.

When the lift hit the second floor, the doors opened and they exited into a plushly carpeted corridor that stretched off to their left. A series of offices stood on either side. Bill stopped outside Room 24 and knocked on the door before pushing it open. Inside was a young guy with short cropped hair, dark eyes and a black and purple Malloy tracksuit. He was sitting at a table stuffing letters into envelopes.

"Anton," Bill announced. "This is Danny. He's here to do some work experience, so show him a good time. He hopes to be a Formula One driver some day."

Danny felt embarrassed. Anton showed no reaction.

"OK," said Bill. "Good luck, lads. Alfie, now we can get cracking on that new project I told you about; I've put the day aside."

Alfie was often involved in projects with various Formula One organizations.

"I'll be back at five-ish for the return journey," said Alfie, giving Danny's shoulder a good-luck squeeze. A few seconds later he and Bill were gone.

"Fancy yourself as the next Coulthard or Hamilton, do you?" said Anton with a sneer, standing up.

"It's just that I do karting and I. . ."

"Whatever," replied Anton. "In here you do what I tell you and that means finishing off these." He pointed to the table, which was heaped with a massive pile of the letters and envelopes.

Danny sat down and had a quick read of the letters. They were Team Malloy fan updates to all of the people who'd elected not to receive the emailed ones. There were thousands. But instead of helping him, Anton sprawled in his chair and started sending text messages. After an hour Danny had only made it through a quarter of the pile.

"Er . . . Anton, fancy giving me a hand?"

"Forget it!" snapped Anton, looking up for a couple of seconds. "I'm working on something far more important."

Yeah, right, thought Danny. The task was monotonous but his brain was filled with all sorts of stuff, like the Granger Cup quarter-final, the spat with Tony and the worrying redundancy letters at home, so the time didn't drag as badly as it could have. Anton didn't lift a finger and at midday, he announced he was going for lunch and disappeared. Danny took out the sandwiches he'd prepared that morning and ate them, followed by an apple. He stuck his head out of the door and checked the corridor. It was empty. He sighed heavily and returned to the task in hand. Anton showed up an hour and a half later and immediately got involved with his phone again.

As the minutes dragged on, though, the job started to become boring, and then more boring, and finally exceedingly boring. It wasn't exactly giving him any real insight into how a Formula One manufacturing team worked. Plus Anton was doing nothing to help him and this drove Danny mad; the guy would win the world's top award for laziness. Danny was hugely relieved when Alfie stuck his head round the door at ten to five.

"All right, Danny?" he asked.

Danny nodded and stood up quickly – delighted his getaway driver had arrived.

"Er . . . maybe see you again Anton," muttered Danny, trying his best to be polite, in spite of the fact that he'd taken a colossal dislike to the guy.

"Whatever," replied Anton without looking up from his phone.

"How was it?" asked Alfie as they walked back to the lift.

"It was . . . OK," responded Danny, not wishing to sound ungrateful, "but a little bit boring. I put letters in envelopes."

Alfie frowned. "That's not what Bill asked Anton to do.

There's no point of you being there if you're just stuck in an office doing admin work."

"It's no big deal," replied Danny, masking his disappointment.

"Look, I'll have a word with Bill and we'll make sure you get to do something more interesting tomorrow," promised Alfie.

"Great," replied Danny, his spirits lifting. Today must have just been his introduction – showing him that not everything in the world of Formula One was glamorous or exciting. No, tomorrow would be a much better day – he was convinced of it. He'd be in Malloy HQ again and this time he'd see some top stuff. Bring it on!

9

Instead of driving Danny home, Alfie headed for Sparks Cross. Forty minutes later Danny was sliding open the huge doors of the shed and making a beeline for his kart.

Wheeling his kart out into the sunshine on a four-wheel rack, he forgot about the boredom of his day at Malloy HQ. Instead he focused on Sunday's race. It wouldn't be like a normal mid-season race day; it would be much more serious than that. Kids from tracks all round the region would be there and some of them were bound to be as good as Danny, if not better.

Danny wheeled his kart down the ramp and on to the track. He'd changed into his dark blue suit, specialized red and black karting boots, and was wearing his rib protector, which was very handy for taking corners hard and prevented a great deal of pain, not to mention rib fractures. He took a deep breath, climbed into the kart

61

and put on his helmet. For most races you had a rolling start; you were already on the move when you came to the start line. But most karts were standing starters nowadays and as soon as he hit the start button, the kart revved to life and shot forward.

Within seconds the flash of exhilaration hit him – a sensation he got every time he drove. Almost instantly, he was hurtling round the track at sixty mph, his vehicle and himself low to the ground, the wind whipping past him. It felt good to be alone on the track and confidence oozed through him. He leant in at the corners and experimented with outside and inside manoeuvres, thinking about Alfie's overtaking DVD.

The back-of-seat transponder – fitted to every kart – was recording the number of laps Danny was driving, his average speed and his fastest lap time. All of this info was uploading on to a laptop in the office. Today, Alfie was in charge of the laptop, but on race days he'd often pass this job to one of the race marshals. Once your drive was finished, you could download all of this info on to your own laptop. It was a brilliant and detailed method for tracking one's progress.

Danny did ten laps and when he pulled off the track he spotted a kart he didn't recognize, standing outside the shed. It was a brand new, gleaming orange vehicle with black stripes on the side pods and some intricate purple patterns on the nose cone and the rear bar. It boasted brand new slicks and sparkling axles. It was a beauty and it must have cost a fortune. But it wasn't just the kart that caught Danny's attention; it was the driver.

Tony Butler.

Danny climbed out of his kart. "What are you doing here?" he demanded angrily, affronted that Tony had shown up at his special place.

"It's a free country," replied Tony with an arrogant shake of his greasy head. "I've been karting for years and I belonged to another club. But when I heard you were a member here I came to check it out. And guess what?"

Danny didn't want to hear the answer.

"I've joined up as a member. So you'll be seeing a lot more of me!"

Danny groaned.

"Is that your kart?" sneered Tony, turning his head towards Danny's vehicle.

"Yeah," snapped Danny sourly.

"Well, this is mine," said Tony, giving his chassis a fond pat. "I think it probably has a few advantages over your rust heap, so feel free to admire it whenever you want."

Danny felt his blood simmering and had to suppress the urge to whack the arrogant invader in the face.

"Oh, there's one other thing," said Tony.

Danny's fists were clenched so tight they hurt.

"What?" he asked.

"I got through the Granger Cup heats at my old club, so I'll be racing against you in the regional quarter-final here on Sunday."

Tony looked at Danny's horrified face and chuckled to himself, before pushing his kart down the slope.

"Why have you let *him* join?" bellowed Danny, storming into Alfie's office, his temples bulging with rage.

Alfie looked up from his computer screen. "Who are you talking about?" he asked with a bewildered expression.

"Him!" cried Danny, pointing out of the window. "Tony Butler!"

"What's he to you?"

"He goes to my school and he's a total pain in the backside. He's always mouthing off in people's faces. He's massive trouble."

Alfie took a deep breath and indicated for Danny to sit down on the chair on the other side of his desk.

"I had no idea you knew him," said Alfie, "and even if I did, I couldn't have stopped him from joining."

"But this is the one place I can get away from him," groaned Danny.

"Look, Danny," said Alfie kindly. "I'm sorry this kid is the bane of your life, I really am. But unfortunately we sometimes have to get along with people we detest – it's just one of those things. We'd be happier if they didn't exist, but they do, and somehow we have to deal with them."

"But he's in the Granger Cup quarter-final. I'll be racing against him!"

"So?"

"Come on, Alfie! Look at his kart! It's straight out of one of the top kart design groups. It's got everything. He'll leave me for dust."

"That's rubbish, Danny, and you know it," said Alfie, his tone switching to "firm" mode. "You'll come across plenty of Tony Butlers with their brand new karts on your travels, and believe me they don't always come out on top. Some of them are their own worst enemies."

"But he'll be hanging out here all the time and hassling me – I can't stand him."

"He won't be hassling you, Danny, because if he does, I'll be on to him before you know it. You're one of my longest-standing members, and I won't let him spoil your time here. Do you get me?"

As he walked up to the bus stop a few minutes later, Danny was pleased he'd talked to Alfie, but it hadn't made him feel that much better about Tony Butler joining Sparks Cross and racing in the Granger Cup quarter-final.

"What's with the face of thunder?" asked Dad when Danny got home. Danny went straight to the fridge and searched for a can of Coke.

"It's nothing," replied Danny sulkily.

"Come on, mate, I know when there's something up. Tell me what it is."

"Why should I?" shouted Danny, whose loud voice clearly surprised his father as well as himself.

"Easy, mate, there's no need to go crazy! You know it's better to get things out than to keep them in and let them fester."

"You keep secrets from me, so I keep secrets from you!" shouted Danny furiously, grabbing the Coke and storming upstairs.

10

The next morning, Danny nipped downstairs, wolfed down a bowl of cereal and then shouted "BYE!" before heading off. He didn't want to see Dad. He knew he'd lost it last night, but Dad being so secretive was really bugging him. Something was definitely up with Dad's work, and Mum knew about it too. Why were they treating him like some little kid and hiding the whole story from him?

A bus was just pulling up at the stop on the main road, so he legged it and just managed to get on. The bus stopped directly outside Malloy HQ. When he went in to reception, Roberta greeted him with a smile, and Alberto, the security guard, made Danny's pass without asking for his name. Danny felt a small surge of pride. At least they knew who he was.

"Mr Moore sends his apologies, but he can't meet you

this morning," said Roberta. "He's asked for you to go to Room 24."

Danny felt a sinking feeling in the pit of his stomach. Room 24? That meant Anton and probably another incredibly boring job. What had happened to Alfie's promise to make sure he did something more interesting?

Anton was in Room 24 with a whole series of paper mountains standing on the table.

"Right," he said delightedly on seeing Danny, "all of these documents need to be filed in those three cabinets over there. Most things are stored electronically, but some documents have to be kept in paper form too."

Danny looked at the thousands of documents and gulped. Just like the day before, as soon as Danny got started, Anton busied himself with sending text messages. As Danny filed away the documents, in his head he was cursing Alfie and Bill Moore for landing him in this rubbish situation, and Anton for being the planet's most repulsive inhabitant.

It took an eternity for midday to arrive, and when it did Anton scooted off again, leaving Danny to eat his sandwiches and feel miserable – alone, in Room 24.

Anton spent ages at lunch and when he came back he just scowled at Danny and sat down with his phone. But ten minutes later there was a knock on the door. Anton moved so fast it was like watching a speeded-up film. He flipped his phone shut, swivelled his chair round to face the desk, grabbed a whole pile of papers and began studying them earnestly. "Come in!" he called in a brisk businesslike tone, making it look like he was totally immersed in his work.

A tall, wiry guy with very thin glasses and an immaculate grey suit poked his head round the door and eyeballed Danny.

"Bill Moore wants you to go to Room 16; it's on the floor below," he announced.

Danny had never stood up faster. He'd have pretty much done anything to get away from Anton and his mind-numbing tasks. But Danny's joy was quickly overridden when he thought about what his next job could be. What if it was *more* boring than the work Anton gave? Could things get worse?

He took the stairs down to the first floor, walked along the corridor and knocked on the door of Room 16.

"COME IN!" boomed a voice.

Danny opened the door and nearly died of complete and utter shock. For there, sitting at one end of a long white conference table, in front of a laptop, was . . . Scot Devlin. He was by himself, and wearing designer jeans, trainers, a black hoodie and a red baseball cap.

For a few seconds Danny just stood there, freaked out

big time. Maybe it was just a hologram of Devlin and not the real thing.

But when Devlin spoke he sounded pretty real.

"You're Danny, right?" he asked.

Danny nodded, trying desperately hard not to show how overwhelmed he felt. He was actually in the same room as Scot Devlin – Carl would be SO jealous!

"Bill Moore mentioned there was someone doing work experience in today," said Devlin, "and I told him I could do with some help in here."

He beckoned for Danny to come over. On trembling legs Danny crossed the room, his heart thudding like a punchbag receiving a battering. He could now see it was most definitely Devlin, but what on earth could the Formula One star want with him?

Devlin reached out his hand and Danny shook it nervously. Devlin then reached to the floor, picked up a gigantic mail sack and tipped its entire contents on to the table. "Fan mail," he grinned.

"Wow!" murmured Danny.

"Some people let their managers deal with all of their correspondence, but I like to keep my hand in," explained Devlin. "I want to know how people respond to me and Formula One racing in general. There's no way I can reply to them all, but I usually pick between five and ten a week – the ones from kids who are seriously ill or grannies who are in hospital, that kind of thing – and reply to them personally."

"Cool," replied Danny.

"I'd like you to act as my filter," said Devlin. "Pick out the ones who could do with a bit of a lift in their lives, and leave them down this end of the table. The others can go back into the sack and my management team will send those people standard replies. Are you OK with that?"

Danny nodded eagerly and sat down to begin the task. Devlin turned to his laptop screen and hit some of the keys. As Danny worked, he shot a couple of sideways glances at Devlin, still finding it hard to believe he was in the same room as the Formula One driver.

After about five minutes, Devlin stood up. "I've got to head out and meet my tech guys," he said, giving Danny a friendly pat on the shoulder. "But I really appreciate you doing this for me."

"No problem," replied Danny.

"Great. Are you here for any more time?"

"I'm doing the next two days."

"Excellent," smiled Devlin, "maybe see you around."

Danny raised his hand and gave Devlin a quick wave.

Devlin smiled back, headed to the door and was gone.

11

"I can't believe you actually MET him!"

Carl and Danny were in the street kicking a football around. Carl's expression hadn't changed in the ten minutes since Danny had broken the news. He looked so shocked that Danny might just as well have informed him that he'd flown to Mars with a jet pack.

"He was standing as near to me as you are now!" declared Danny, still getting used to that fact. It was only a couple of days ago that they'd watched Devlin burn up the track at the F-NEX Arena.

"Did he say anything about your Formula One prospects? Is he looking for a new manager?"

Danny laughed. "I was only with him for about five minutes so we didn't get to talk properly, but he was well cool."

"You are SO lucky," said Carl, trapping the ball on his

chest and volleying it back to Danny. "Do you think you'll meet him again?"

"No idea," replied Danny, whacking it back. "I wish I'd thought of getting his autograph, though!"

"If you do see him again, don't forget to get an autograph for me too!"

"Trust me," winked Danny.

Carl stayed for supper, and all he and Danny could talk about was Scot Devlin.

"A few days ago he was just a figure on a TV screen," said Carl, "and now Danny's hanging out with him. Incredible!"

"I didn't exactly hang out with him," cut in Danny, who, although completely thrilled by events, didn't want to overexaggerate what had happened.

"As good as," said Carl.

"Are you two going to be famous?" asked Katie, spooning some beans into her mouth.

"Maybe," said Carl, "but only if I handle my client carefully." He pointed a thumb at Danny.

Danny laughed.

Carl stayed for a bit after supper and then headed home. Danny lay down on his bed and closed his eyes. He pictured Room 16, the letters and Devlin himself. Alfie had really delivered now. Even meeting Devlin for five minutes made the work experience at Malloy HQ one hundred per cent worthwhile.

He was about to have a shower and get ready for bed when he heard his parents talking in low voices out in the back garden. He walked to his bedroom window and looked out. Dad was holding up a letter for Mum to see. Dad looked crestfallen. Mum raised her voice a bit but Dad put a finger to his lips for her to keep quiet. He crumpled up the paper and chucked it in the wheelie bin at the side of the house.

Danny suddenly felt a lightning bolt of determination. This was the third time he'd seen weird behaviour over a letter and he was now absolutely convinced that Dad was about to lose his job. He'd seen his parents' faces. Both of them looked totally despairing. Mum taking on more bookkeeping would bring in a bit of extra cash, but it wouldn't be enough. Jobs weren't easy to come by and all Dad had ever done was be a postman. Fixing up cars didn't pay enough to be anything other than a hobby. What if Dad couldn't find another job? Danny would have to forget karting completely. They'd never be able to stretch to even the most basic fuel and maintenance costs.

He turned off his bedroom light and sat in darkness, the dread growing in his chest. He heard his parents go up to bed and waited until they turned off their bedroom lights. He gave it another fifteen minutes and then crept downstairs. Padding across the kitchen, he slowly pulled back the two bolts on the kitchen door. He opened it a centimetre at a time and when there was a big enough gap, slid through.

Out in the yard he took a quick look up at his parents' bedroom. The lights were off. He tiptoed over to the wheelie bin and very gently tilted it towards him. The bin was fairly full and the envelope was nestling on top of a black bin bag.

Danny retrieved the envelope and carefully stood the wheelie bin upright again. He felt a tremor of nerves. How bad was the news contained within going to be? Was Dad going to be made redundant without any compensation? Was he already looking for another job? Would they have to move immediately?

He hurried back inside, locked the kitchen door and went back to his room. He sat down on his bed, turned his bedside light on and lifted the flap of the envelope. He held the letter up for a couple of seconds, then unfolded it and read.

Jeff Young
Commercial & Marketing Director
Full Click Electronics Group

Dear Mr Sharp

Thank you very much for your letter of May 7th regarding possible sponsorship for your son, Danny, and his karting aspirations. Unfortunately we receive thousands of such letters and can only select one driver per year. I'm afraid that Danny isn't one of these. I know this response must be disappointing and I wish you and your son every success finding sponsorship elsewhere.

Yours sincerely

Jeff Young

In an instant Danny was outside his parents' bedroom, hammering on their door with his fists. The door flew open and Dad stumbled out, rubbing his eyes.

"What is it, Danny?" he blurted out. "Is it Katie; is she OK?"

"Katie's fine," shouted Danny. "It's about this!"

He held up the crumpled letter in front of his father's face, bubbling with rage. Dad had been seeking sponsorship behind his back! How could he? He'd always said they were in this together!

"Oh," said Dad.

"What's going on?" Danny demanded.

Dad pulled the bedroom door shut. "Let's go downstairs and talk," he whispered.

A minute later they were in the kitchen. Dad made

himself a cup of tea. "Do you want one?" he asked.

Danny shook his head.

"Look," said Dad, sitting down and cradling the mug in his hands. "I'm sorry you had to find out about it this way."

"Well, if you'd told me you'd started looking for sponsorship I wouldn't have had to go scavenging around in the bin, would I?" said Danny angrily. "You lied to me. You said we weren't ready to seek a sponsor yet. I thought those letters were about you being made redundant. I thought we'd have to sell the house and move!"

"I'm sorry," said Dad. "I did lie to you, but I was only trying to protect you. It's such a competitive world out there and I didn't want you to get down with every rejection I received."

"I don't need protecting," snapped Danny.

"Fine," said Dad. "I'll keep you in the loop from now on."

"Too right!" nodded Danny.

There was a pause.

"How many companies have you contacted?" asked Danny.

"At this stage, just twenty," replied Dad, taking a sip of his tea.

"Twenty! How many have got back to you?"

"That was the twentieth."

"And they've all said no?"

Dad nodded. "But twenty is nothing, mate," he said. "There are hundreds and hundreds of companies and organizations out there who offer sponsorship money. It's just a case of finding the right one. We'll get there; I know we will."

Danny was hugely relieved that Dad wasn't about to lose his job – he could probably get new karting gloves now – but he was crushed that every letter had been a rejection. He wasn't going to admit that, though, because then Dad would say he'd been right not to tell him. "So there are other people we can try?" said Danny.

"Absolutely," nodded Dad. "I'll hit the next group at the weekend."

"And you'll tell me exactly who you're contacting from now on?"

"I promise. I just had this idea that one of the twenty would say yes and then I'd be able to surprise you with fantastic news."

Danny managed a small smile. "That would have been great," he admitted.

Dad sank the last dregs of his tea, rinsed out the mug and put it on the draining board. "Come on, let's get some sleep."

Danny nodded and they walked back upstairs together.

Mum was standing at the top of the stairs. "We didn't mean to keep the letters a secret from you, but we didn't want you to see the rejections," she said.

"I know," said Danny. "Dad's explained it. I much prefer knowing."

"I told him – we'll get a sponsor soon," grinned Dad. "It won't be long before those first twenty will be kicking themselves for turning us down!"

"I agree," smiled Mum. "And from now on, if Dad writes any more letters and gets any replies, we'll let you know."

"OK," said Danny.

"That's settled, then," said Dad.

"Night," said Mum.

"Night," replied Dad, heading back to his bedroom.

He sat on his floor of his room for a bit, flicking through some old Formula One magazines. If only someone important would show up at Sparks Cross one day and catch him putting his kart through its paces. Maybe they'd be impressed enough to chuck some sponsorship money in his direction. That would be perfect. He could really do up his kart or even buy a brand new one!

And then he remembered he'd be back at Malloy HQ tomorrow. Maybe he'd get a chance to help out Scot Devlin again. All of these possibilities fired optimism into

Danny's heart and he went to sleep that night willing the next day to arrive.

12

Bill Moore was waiting at reception for Danny the next morning.

"Excellent to see you!" he beamed, giving Danny a hearty handshake.

Alberto handed Danny his badge and Danny quickly followed Bill, who was marching over to the lift. "First stop, Room 24," announced Bill.

Danny's heart plummeted. Please – no more Anton!

A couple of minutes later, Bill pushed open the door of Room 24. Anton was sitting at the table in front of a huge stack of cardboard cut-out kits.

"These are for prize-winners of a competition we ran," explained Bill. "The pieces come in sheets and they have to be separated and bundled into kits before we send them. Isn't that right, Anton?"

Anton nodded with a smug grin on his face; he knew

cheap labour when he saw it and he'd earmarked Danny to complete this mind-numbing job for him.

But Bill had other plans.

"Two quick things, Anton," said Bill. "First, a gigantic box with the remaining cardboard sections is waiting for you in reception. And second, you won't be able to make use of Danny's services this morning."

Anton's face sank so low Danny was sure his chin would reach the carpet.

"Come on, Danny," said Bill, sweeping out of the room.

They caught the lift to the basement and walked out into a long corridor illuminated by strips of fluorescent orange light. At the end of the corridor were steel double doors bearing a sign stating: ABSOLUTELY NO ENTRY EXCEPT FOR AUTHORIZED PERSONNEL!

Danny watched as Bill punched a number code into a metallic wall panel and the doors buzzed open. They walked through into another corridor, this one much shorter, that led outside. As they emerged into the daylight, excitement coursed through Danny's veins. They were out on the practice track. This was excellent! But not only that: Scot Devlin and four of his tech team were standing by a workbench ten metres to the left, locked in a deep technical discussion.

When Scot saw them approaching he shouted out,

"It's marketing man Bill Moore and my fan-mail filter guy!"

Danny couldn't believe it; Devlin was referring to *him*!

Danny and Bill walked over and the tech team guys, all of whom were wearing black and purple Malloy sweatshirts, nodded their hellos.

"This is Danny," said Bill, "a promising young kart driver, who has hopes of making it to Formula One. He's here to see how this place works. He helped out Scot yesterday. Would any of you mind if he sits in on your discussion?"

"Not at all," said a guy with a beanie hat.

"This is Dave Corby," said Bill, pointing to the beanie hat guy. "He's the leader of this team, and these guys are Rick, Sanjay and Gary."

Danny gave them all a nervous smile.

"We're doing some work on the steering wheel," explained Devlin, beckoning Danny over to stand next to him. A huge and technical drawing of a steering wheel and steering column was spread out on a square table. Danny walked over, his forehead perspiring at the prospect of being so near his Formula One hero again. He forced himself to take his eyes off Devlin and focus on the diagram. The wheel was a beautiful sight: a vast array of gleaming buttons, knobs and dials.

"The problem we're having," explained Devlin, "is

with changing brake pressure, which is controlled by that dial there. It's out just a fraction, but that could cost me a race."

"That wheel must have cost at least forty grand," murmured Danny.

"You're very close," said Dave, looking impressed.

"Is that one the fuel-air adjuster and that one the rev limiter?" asked Danny, pointing out another couple of dials on the diagram, surprising himself that he had the courage to speak.

Devlin raised an eyebrow. "So you know a bit about Formula One cars, then?"

Danny blushed. "A little," he replied modestly.

"When did you get interested?" asked Devlin.

Danny felt very self-conscious with all of them looking at him, but he went on. "My dad got me into cars when I was really young. I've followed the Grand Prix circuit ever since I can remember."

"So, you're a serious fan?" asked Devlin.

"Er . . . yes!" grinned Danny, delighted that Scot Devlin was taking an interest in him.

"Well, that's what we like to see, isn't it, lads!" smiled Devlin at his team. Dave and the others nodded. "Now, let's see what we can do about this brake pressure."

Danny had read that Devlin liked to be involved with every aspect of his car and race preparation, and the next two and a half hours bore this out. Dave and Sanjay carried out the actual steering wheel. It had looked great on the diagram, but in the flesh it was one hundred times more impressive. As the tech team started working on hundreds of wires and connections in the wheel, Devlin was in the thick of it, asking questions, making suggestions and generally getting stuck in. Danny stayed as close to the action as possible. It was incredible!

When midday arrived, the team downed tools and went off to the cafeteria to get some lunch. But Devlin didn't move. He sat down on a bench. Danny wasn't sure what he was supposed to do – he was alone again with Scot Devlin. It was surreal. But after a few seconds of indecision, he sat down on the bench too.

Neither of them said anything for at least a minute, and when the silence was beginning to become awkward, Devlin spoke.

"How badly do you want to become a Formula One driver?" he asked, without looking at Danny.

"Really badly," replied Danny. "I mean, whenever I have any free time, I go to Sparks Cross – that's my karting club – and practise or work on my kart."

"Do you think about karting when you're not there?"

"All the time. I even dream about it!"

Devlin nodded.

"Seriously!" went on Danny. "I just wish the years

could speed up and I could be ready to drive in Formula One."

"I was exactly the same at your age," said Devlin wistfully. "I lived and breathed for karting, and guess what? Now I live and breathe for Formula One racing. Once it's in your blood and bones; that's it, isn't it?"

It was Danny's turn to nod.

"I remember being about six and looking into the shop window of this kart store near where I grew up," continued Devlin. "All I wanted to do was sit in one of the karts and take off, you know, head for the moon!"

Danny laughed.

"But I have to warn you, Danny. Making it to Formula One is an incredibly tough journey. You'll face loads of setbacks, from teammates and coaches, manufacturers, fellow drivers and sponsors. It's not all smooth sailing; there are a lot of sharks out there. There will be times when you think about giving up. Your spirits will get crushed on more than one occasion. Do you get what I'm saying?"

Danny nodded solemnly, drinking in every word. He pulled out a piece of paper and a pen. "Thanks for the advice. Could you do an autograph for me and my best mate, Carl?" he asked hesitantly.

"Sure!" smiled Devlin, taking the pen and committing his signature to paper, twice.

"Right," said Devlin, jumping up. "I'm doing a watch advert this afternoon in Geneva and I need to make tracks to the airport. I'll be back late tonight. You're in tomorrow, aren't you?"

Danny nodded. "It's my last day."

"OK, I'm sure I'll see you around then."

Devlin broke into a jog, and a few moments later, he disappeared inside the building. Danny sat on the bench for over ten minutes, spooling back and replaying the whole conversation.

I was exactly the same at your age.

Danny felt like he was walking on a cloud for the rest of the day and even when he had to work "with" Anton in the afternoon, sticking financial data into press packs, he didn't care. He'd had a one-to-one conversation with the world's fastest-rising Formula One star and no one could ever take that away from him!

That night, Danny spent over an hour on the phone to Carl, going over and over the time he'd spent with Devlin and his tech team.

"This is the most amazing thing that has ever happened," enthused Carl. "Did you get the autographs?"

"Of course!" laughed Danny.

"Brilliant!" shouted Carl. "Did you mention that if he ever gets sick of his management, then I'll step in?"

"I thought that was a bit much," replied Danny.

"Fair enough," conceded Carl, "but if he ever mentions it in future, don't forget about me."

"Of course not."

Danny was up at six the following morning, having slept very lightly. Today was the last of his four days at Malloy and he intended to make the most of it. He hoped that today would be as brilliant as yesterday.

But on arrival at HQ, Roberta directed him straight up to Room 24. As he went up in the lift, he hoped that Bill Moore would be there to whisk him away from the demanding and sour clutches of Anton. But when he arrived the room was empty.

However, there was a brief note on the table from Anton, explaining that three separate emails had to be sent out to three hundred people but they couldn't be sent out as group emails, so Danny would have to track down each individual address. The task was excruciatingly boring and took up the entire morning and the early part of the afternoon. But just as the boredom was threatening to overpower him, the phone on the desk went. Danny waited for a few rings and then picked it up.

"Danny? It's Bill Moore. I'm sorry you've been up in Room 24 again. Could you come to reception, please?"

Danny didn't hesitate. He was out of the room in five seconds and hurrying downstairs. Bill was there and once again Danny was led into the belly of the building and out on to the practice track. To his delight, Scot and the tech team were there again. But this time, instead of just the steering wheel and steering column, a complete Malloy Formula One car was parked on the practice track.

"Hey, Danny!" called out Devlin, when he saw Danny and Bill approaching. "Come over here!"

Danny was amazed. He'd only met Devlin twice but already the guy was treating him like a trusted aide. They walked over and stopped beside Devlin and his crew.

Danny's eyes swivelled from Devlin to the car. He thought he'd been close to one at the F-NEX Arena, but this was a different world altogether. It was just *metres* away from him. He had to stop himself from running forward and throwing himself on to it. That might look a bit too enthusiastic!

It was a sleek black and purple beast, glinting in the afternoon sunshine. The car had a mid-engine, and an open cockpit with a chassis mainly made of carbon fibre composites. It had multi-link suspension with pushrod-operated springs and dampers on the chassis. It was fitted with gleaming slick tyres and carbon fibre disc brakes; these features helped to keep the vehicle's weight down to a minimum.

It was a magnificent creation.

"We replaced the steering wheel," said Devlin, facing Danny, "and in a minute, I'm going to put this little beauty through its paces. My crew are going to be taking a close look at the car's progress, but I want you to be trackside, OK?"

Danny nodded and Devlin indicated for Danny to

follow him. So while Bill and the tech team stayed where they were, Danny and Devlin climbed down the ten steps leading to the track. They were now standing less than a metre away from the car.

"Before I drive, I think you should get a chance to sit in a real Formula One car," smiled Devlin. "I can promise you it will feel way different to sitting in a kart!"

A few seconds later, Devlin was helping Danny climb into the cockpit. He sat down slowly, his body sinking into the suede seat. The steering wheel was too far in front of him to reach it, so he moved to the front edge of the seat and gripped it. He closed his eyes for a few seconds and imagined he was on the track at Monte Carlo, speeding past his rivals, taking pole position, appreciating the screams and cheers of the spectators urging him on.

"What do you reckon?" asked Devlin.

"It's . . . it's incredible!" breathed Danny.

"OK," said Devlin, leaning forward to help Danny out of the vehicle. "I'm taking her out for some laps now. Take everything in; the speed, the track, the smell. Get a real feel for it!"

With that, Devlin gave him a wink and climbed into the vehicle. Danny's head was whirring. He'd just sat in Scot Devlin's car and now he was going to watch him drive at point-blank range.

A few minutes later, Devlin was powering round the straights and the bends, experimenting with harder and softer braking and going inside and outside on corners. He was a speeding smudge of purple and black. The noise was incredible.

Danny loved every second of it – he was in his own personal stadium getting a one-to-one session with a serious contender for world champion. He could have stayed and watched him for hours, but after twenty minutes Devlin pulled the car in to the side of the track and got out. Danny ran towards him.

"How did I do?" asked Devlin, taking off his helmet.

"You were amazing!" gushed Danny. "Those corners were fantastic. It's how I dream of driving! But it'll take me years to be able to take a track like that!"

"You never know," smiled Devlin. "Put in the hours and you might get there sooner than you think."

They walked up the stairs and joined the others.

"How did it feel to be out there?" asked Bill.

"It was awesome!" replied Danny.

"He's not bad, is he?" joked Rick, jerking his head in Devlin's direction. Devlin laughed and nudged Rick in the ribs.

"Joking aside," said Devlin, "it's a constant learning curve. Every time I'm out on the track it's a new experience. And I've got these guys constantly feeding me info. All drivers, whatever stage they're at, need to take other people's suggestions on board. There's no room for complacency in this sport."

On hearing these words, an image suddenly flickered into Danny's mind. "Er . . . you know this year's Malaysian Grand Prix?" he said.

Devlin and the others nodded.

Danny bit his bottom lip. Being here with Devlin and the crew had gone to his head a bit and Alfie's advice about overtaking was flooding through his brain. Plus, hadn't Devlin just said that drivers, whoever they were, had to listen to suggestions?

"Well . . . you . . . you could have grabbed second place if you'd overtaken Antonio Gallance on the third to last bend. Shouldn't you have gone outside?"

Devlin's smile vanished. Tony coughed. The other crew members exchanged surprised glances.

"I think that's overstepping the mark, Danny," said Bill Moore sternly. He looked angry; his cheeks had gone red.

Danny was aghast. "I . . . er . . . I . . . just. . ."

"That's enough for today, Danny. I think it's time you went home." said Bill firmly.

14

Danny ran. Down the steps he raced and along the side of the track, hot tears streaming down his face.

He cringed as he replayed Bill's words in his head.

I think that's overstepping the mark, Danny.

What had he *done*? Scot Devlin had allowed him to get right up close, to the car, to the track, to the tech team and to the man himself. And now he'd gone and completely blown it by speaking out of turn. What had possessed him to say it? Who was he to lecture Scot Devlin about the Malaysian Grand Prix? Bill had been the one to say something, but Danny had seen from Devlin's expression that he also hadn't been impressed by the schoolboy stupidity of the comment. And Bill would surely tell Alfie and would probably never let him come near this place again!

With an agonizing feeling in his chest, Danny saw a

side door open and went through it back into the building. He took a left without thinking about where he was going. He saw someone coming towards him and kept his head down, wiping away the tears. He crashed through a set of double doors, up a short flight of steps and along a tiled corridor. He finally stopped by a stairwell and leant against a pillar. His breathing was heavy, his heart was rocketing, his brain ached. How was he going to tell anyone about this? Mum, Dad, Carl? He couldn't face it.

He stared miserably out of the window and found himself facing a small car park that was flanked by potted bushes. The car that stood out was a yellow Porsche 911 Turbo, a vehicle he knew well. It was Scot Devlin's "run-around" and had featured in loads of magazines. The turbo's spec was seriously impressive. It had a 3.8-litre direct-injected flat 6 engine, wheel-mounted paddles and the Porsche Traction Management System that distributed torque between the front and rear differentials via an electronic multi-plate clutch.

But it wasn't just the Porsche he found himself looking at. It was the man who was crouching down by the driver's door pulling a short, thin, metallic object out of his jacket pocket and inserting it into the lock on the driver's side. The man had his back to Danny so he couldn't see his face. Danny choked back the tears and pressed his face against the window, intrigued by the spectacle. And then the man turned round for a brief moment just to check that no one was watching him. Danny's heart felt a sharp pulse. It was Vince Dutton – the greasy journalist who'd angered Devlin so much at the F-NEX Arena; the guy Dad said would do anything to get some dirt on Malloy or any of its drivers.

He'll bite people's heads off if he's paid enough. He's a nasty piece of work.

Danny's mouth opened in shock. Vince Dutton was breaking into Scot Devlin's car!

Without thinking, Danny started moving. Down the stairs he ran, finding himself in another corridor on the ground floor. He ran on, catching a glimpse of Dutton out of a window. The guy was now actually inside Devlin's car.

Pushing open a fire exit, Danny crouched down and crept forward behind the covering of some bushes. He stopped when he was fewer than ten metres away from the Porsche. Raising his head a few centimetres he watched as Dutton quickly reached for some documents from the back seat of the car. He pulled out a tiny digital camera and quickly photographed them, looking round again to make sure he wasn't being observed. Danny quickly dipped his head out of sight. Dutton then replaced the papers, shut the car door, locked the vehicle and stood up as if absolutely nothing had happened. He took a few steps away from the Porsche and speed-dialled a number on his mobile.

He talked in a hushed whisper, so Danny couldn't hear much, but there were certain things his ears did detect: "*The Klaxon deal . . . inflated prices . . . official inquiry.*"

None of it made any sense to Danny, but at this stage that didn't bother him; what bothered him was that a hostile journalist had just broken into Scot Devlin's car, with the clear intention of causing Devlin trouble. However much of a fool he'd been back there, he needed to find Devlin as soon as possible to tell him what had just happened.

By the time he stood up, Dutton was gone, so Danny hurriedly retraced his steps. When he reached the tunnel leading out to the practice track, he was faced by the metallic security panel on the wall. Luckily he'd taken a good look when Bill Moore had tapped in the entry code – 2634 – so he quickly hit those keys and the door opened. He hurried forward, planning the speech he was about to make in his head.

But as he emerged outside he froze in his tracks. The place was now completely empty.

Everyone was gone.

15

Danny raced back inside, his legs pumping and his brain going into overdrive. He needed to warn Devlin about the Porsche break-in ASAP. Dutton was probably planning to write some kind of a damning story about him in the papers. It could be something that might hamper or even ruin Scot Devlin's career.

He sprinted on, down a passageway and past a couple of conference rooms. A minute later he found himself at the same window looking down on to the car park. The good news was that the yellow Porsche was still there; the bad news was that Scot Devlin was striding towards it.

Danny darted down the stairs, determined to get to Devlin before he took flight. He'd show him that he wasn't just some kid who thought he knew it all. He had vital info for Devlin and Devlin would surely be grateful.

Maybe then Devlin would give him another chance if he promised not to give him any more driving advice.

Once again, he burst through the emergency exit, except this time, instead of hiding behind the bushes, he pelted across the asphalt, making a beeline for the Porsche. When he was less than twenty metres away the engine revved up. Danny increased his pace and started waving his arms to get Devlin's attention. He was now just ten metres away. But as he closed in on the vehicle, Devlin floored the accelerator and the car shot out of the car park, kicking up a thick cloud of dust.

"STOP!" Danny yelled after the vehicle. But it was too late. With another burst of acceleration, the Porsche spun round the corner and out of sight.

"So let me get this straight," said Carl, his face contorted with amazement. "You got to sit – to actually sit – in Devlin's Formula One car, this Bill Moore guy tells you off for overstepping the mark, then you see Vince Dutton breaking into Devlin's Porsche?"

"I know it sounds unbelievable," nodded Danny, "but that's exactly what happened. I blew it big time with Devlin!"

They were sitting on a bench in the park. It was eight-thirty p.m. and the light was slowly starting to fade.

"You didn't blow it with Devlin!" replied Carl, popping

a chocolate into his mouth. "It was Bill who said something, not Devlin. Anyway, Devlin *should* have overtaken Gallance on that bend in the Malaysian Grand Prix. He probably listened to you and took it on board. He's bound to know a genius Formula One mind like yours when he sees one."

Danny smiled; the first time he'd smiled for hours. Carl could always make him see the positive side of things.

"Either way, I've got to let Devlin know about Dutton breaking into his car. I only heard a bit of what Dutton was saying. It was *The Klaxon deal . . . inflated prices . . . official inquiry.* Do you have any idea what that's about?"

"Nope," replied Carl with a shrug of his shoulders.

Before Danny could say anything else, another voice cut through the air. "Look, if it isn't the bad losers!"

Danny groaned: Tony Butler. Why couldn't the guy just leave him alone? Tony was with Kev and some of his other mates. Tony peeled away from his crowd and strolled over to Danny and Carl.

"What do you want?" snapped Danny irritably.

"Ooh! Do I detect a little bit of a temper?" taunted Tony.

"Go away, Tony," said Carl, quietly but firmly.

"I'm not staying long," announced Tony with a false smile. "I've just come to say that after your cheating – I mean, your last-minute basket, you won't be so lucky on the track at Sparks Cross."

"Yeah, yeah," replied Danny scornfully.

"I can't wait to race my speed machine against your, er . . . vehicle."

"You're pathetic, Tony!" snarled Danny.

"Say what you like," Tony replied, shrugging, "but it will be me, not you, who qualifies for the Granger Cup semis."

"In your dreams," muttered Danny angrily.

"You'll see," smirked Tony, before sauntering back to his mates.

"I hate him!" hissed Danny.

"Don't let him get to you," said Carl, "he's just an irritating idiot."

But half an hour later when they walked home, Danny was still trying to unwind himself from Tony's comments. If only he could just brush them away like Carl. Maybe that would happen in the future, but with the Granger Cup heat so close, it certainly wasn't going to happen tonight.

"This is mad, Danny!"

Carl and Danny were on a bus. They'd travelled through the centre of town and were now heading out to the leafy suburbs. Danny had called round at Carl's early that morning to explain his plan.

"I've got to go to Scot Devlin's house and tell him what happened," Danny had explained. "It's the simplest way."

Danny was still smarting from the trackside incident yesterday, but he was trying to put it to the back of his mind and concentrate on letting Devlin know about Vince Dutton's car break-in.

"What," Carl had responded, "you'll just march up to his front door and say, 'Hi, Scot, I'm the kid from Malloy HQ – the one who gave you the driving advice yesterday – well, I saw some sleazy guy break into your car and I thought I should tell you'?"

"Something like that," Danny had replied. "It should be pretty easy."

Carl hadn't been so sure. In fact, he'd been pretty nervous about the whole thing, imagining scores of police officers arresting them for stalking the Formula One star.

"This is his street!" exclaimed Danny, pointing out of the window. The bus eased to a stop. Danny grabbed Carl by the elbow and led him off the bus. They alighted on a very wide tree-lined avenue where every house was detached and worth millions. A couple of footballers lived on this road, as well as a fading film star and a TV quiz-show host.

"And you're really sure about doing this?" asked Carl.

"It's the quickest and most direct route to him," insisted Danny.

"Well, I don't like it," said Carl, checking both ways down the street, in case hordes of police officers were already advancing towards them, riot shields clasped in front of them.

But the street was empty and they were now standing directly in front of Devlin's house. It was a monstrously large mock Tudor mansion, with twelve bedrooms, a swimming pool, a computer games arcade and a cinema. Danny had seen shots of it in the papers. In an attempt to keep out the paparazzi, the Formula One star had planted a line of huge trees at the front of the house and a high metal wall at the back. Even though the trees were incredibly tightly packed, you could catch glimpses of the house through tiny gaps: an ornate staircase here, a chandelier there. On the drive was Devlin's yellow Porsche. Large CCTV cameras were mounted at several points on the walls of the house.

"Come on," said Danny, walking over to the high metallic black gates, attached at each side to a tall brick pillar. There was a small intercom panel on one of the pillars. Danny pressed the buzzer and waited; nothing.

Danny pressed it again; still nothing.

"Let's go," said Carl, looking nervously over his shoulder.

Danny ignored him and pressed the buzzer a third time. For ten seconds nothing happened, but then the intercom crackled into life.

"Hello?"

It was a woman's voice with a slight accent, maybe Eastern European. A housekeeper?

"I have a message for Scot Devlin," said Danny.

"All press enquiries go through his agent," said the voice curtly.

"I'm not from the press," said Danny. "It's . . . personal."

There was a pause. "Is it important?"

"I think so . . . yes, it is important."

Another pause. "What do you want me to do?"

"Could you pass it on to Scot?"

A pause again. "I don't normally speak to fans."

"I'm not a fan . . . well, I am . . . but I have a message for Scot that's not to do with me being a fan. It's vital he reads it, I promise you."

A deep sigh. "OK, I will come out to get it."

"Have you got a bit of paper and a pen?" Danny asked Carl urgently.

Carl rustled around in his jacket pocket and pulled out both items. Danny took them gratefully and quickly scribbled down a message.

To Scot Devlin

At Malloy HQ yesterday, after I overstepped the mark (I'm really sorry, it was stupid) I saw the journalist Vince Dutton break into your yellow Porsche. He looked at some documents, put them back and then spoke on the phone to someone about "the Klaxon deal . . . inflated prices . . . official inquiry." I figured you better know about this.

Danny Sharp

He'd just finished writing when the large oak front door opened and a tall woman with green eyes and light brown scraped-back hair, wearing a white trouser suit, strode purposefully up the carriage drive. She stopped when she got to the gates, and eyed Danny and Carl up and down. She clearly wasn't impressed by the casualness of their dress sense or by the piece of paper Danny slipped through the bars. But she didn't scrunch it up, at least not in their sight. She nodded very slightly, turned round and retreated inside the house.

"Do you think she'll give it to him?" asked Carl, checking that their movements weren't being surveyed.

"She better," replied Danny, as they walked away from the mansion.

17

On the bus journey home, Danny's brain spun. If the woman did give the note to Devlin, maybe he'd be pleased and forget about the embarrassing trackside incident at Malloy HQ; but then again, maybe not?

"When you make it big," said Carl, interrupting Danny's thoughts, "you'll only go to other drivers' houses when you're invited, OK?"

A short while later the bus stopped near the bottom of their estate. Carl hopped off. "Aren't you coming?" he asked.

Danny shook his head. "I'm going over to Sparks Cross to chat to Alfie; calm my nerves before the race."

"Cool," nodded Carl, "speak to you later."

Half an hour later, Danny was sitting in Alfie Price's office. He'd expected Alfie to immediately say that Bill Moore had phoned him about Danny's ridiculous "advice" to Scot Devlin, but Alfie hadn't mentioned it, so Danny wasn't going to either. Two younger boys were out on the track, doing practice runs in the very basic club karts. The boys' dads were both out there too, shouting out encouragement and watching their sons' every twist and turn on the track.

"How are you feeling about tomorrow?" asked Alfie, sitting down on his office chair and spreading his palms out on the desk.

"I'm excited," replied Danny, "and . . . really nervous. It's the biggest race I've ever been in and I don't want to blow it."

"There's no reason why you should blow it," counselled Alfie. "Your preparation has been spot on. That's the great thing about you; you take the sport seriously, and you really want to make a career out of it. Lots of kids dream of success but don't put their backs into the hard work – you do the work, and more."

Danny felt his insides relax a little; once again, a few words from Alfie had put him at his ease.

"Those lads out there are going to be finishing in ten minutes," said Alfie. "Why don't you go and get yourself sorted and do some practice laps?"

"That's exactly what I was going to do," said Danny.

He walked out of the office and sauntered towards the shed. The kids were heading round the track at fairly low speeds. It hadn't been long ago that Danny was driving at that kind of speed. He reached the shed and pulled open the door. Flicking on the lights, he walked down the row of karts until he approached his.

But the second he saw it, his blood turned to ice.

His kart was there.

But it was completely smashed up.

18

Danny stared in horror at his kart. The nose cone, side pods and rear bar had taken a battering; the brake and secondary brake had been bent out of shape.

Two words instantly shot through Danny Sharp's mind. *Tony Butler.*

With a frantically pounding heart, he ran back to Alfie's office and burst through the door. Alfie was on the phone, but seeing Danny's agitated face he quickly killed the call.

"Hey, Danny, what's up?"

"It's my kart!" Danny blurted out. "It's been smashed up!"

Alfie was out of his seat in a second and running over to the shed with Danny. A minute later they were inspecting the damage. Alfie's face had gone taut and pale. Danny had never seen him look like that before.

"Joyriders," said Alfie furiously. He pointed to one of the club's karts and Danny saw that it too had been damaged, although not as badly as his.

"Something like this happened a few years back," said Alfie. "Some kids broke in at night, drove three cars and left them on the track in a terrible state. The police came and said they couldn't do anything about it – it didn't rank high enough up their list of priorities, what with murders and robberies happening."

Danny said nothing. His blood was steaming; he was totally convinced that this wasn't some kids mucking about – it had to be Tony Butler. He must have smashed up the other kart to make it look like he wasn't just targeting Danny's.

Alfie turned to face Danny. "Know any kids who do this sort of thing?" he asked.

For a couple of seconds, Danny considered telling Alfie of his suspicions, but he quickly changed his mind. Pointing his finger at Tony would lead to Alfie investigating and causing Tony loads of hassle. If that happened, there'd be come-back on Danny. No, he had to keep his accusations to himself, at least for the minute.

"No," replied Danny quietly, "but I guess my chances of reaching the semis have gone down to zero."

Alfie gave him a long, hard stare. "You're not going to give up that easily, are you?"

"What else can I do?" snapped Danny. "It's over."

"You'll have to race on one of the club's karts."

"The club's karts are rubbish."

"No, they're not. Some of them are pretty decent. You'd stand a chance."

Danny shook his head miserably. He suddenly wanted Dad here, right now. He dialled home and his father answered on the third ring.

"Dad, it's me. Can you get down to Sparks Cross?"

"What, now? Why?"

"It's my kart. It's been smashed up."

"You're not serious?"

"It's in a terrible way. Can you come now?"

Half an hour later, Danny's father strode up towards the kart shed, disbelief and concern on his face. Danny ran over to greet him. Alfie nodded a grave-faced greeting.

"What happened?" asked Dad.

"I . . . I don't know," said Danny, his voice quivering.

They went inside and as soon as he saw the state of the kart, Dad's face was covered in rage. "Who the hell would do this?" he demanded. "I'd love to wring their necks! It's completely disgraceful!"

Dad didn't often get worked up, but Danny could see from his reddened cheeks and piercing eyes that he was very, very angry.

"Most probably some local kids," answered Alfie. "It's

happened before. I got better locks, but they still find a way to smash them. They break in, drive for a bit and then trash the karts. Except this time for some reason, they didn't even bother to drive them. They just trashed them."

"Have you phoned the police?" asked Dad.

"There's not much point," replied Alfie. "They won't have the time or resources to look into it. And we don't have CCTV. I'm really sorry."

The three of them stood in silence trying to take in the spectacle that faced them.

"OK," Dad sighed heavily. "The damage has been done. We can't turn back time and wish it hadn't happened. We need to go home and plot our next move, Danny. There's no way you're going to miss tomorrow's race."

Danny said nothing; as far as he was concerned, the race was dust.

Mum and Katie were outside the front door waiting for them. Katie had clearly been crying. She ran up to Danny and hugged him tightly.

"Come on in," said Mum, putting her arm round Danny's shoulder. "You've had a terrible shock. Who would do something like this?"

Danny, Katie and Dad sat at the kitchen table while Mum ladled out four bowls of spaghetti bolognese. Danny looked down at the food. He wasn't hungry.

But then Mum fixed her eyes on him and spoke. "Listen, Danny," she began, "there's something I need to tell you." Her tone sounded serious.

Danny looked up. What was this – more bad news?

"Over the years, whenever I could, I've been putting small amounts of money aside – a bit for you and a bit for Katie."

Dad raised his eyebrows. Danny could tell he was surprised Mum was saying this, too.

"The money is meant to be for your education. I hope that one day you both go to college or university and I know how expensive it is. So I wanted to save a bit to help you if you ever choose that path."

Danny tried to speak but his throat was dry.

"I know you think I'm an old fusspot worrying about you having accidents in that kart of yours, but I can't help it. I'm your mother – I'm programmed to worry. And you do go seventy miles an hour in that kart! That's why I never come to see you race. I can't bear to see my little boy hurtling round the track."

"MUM!" complained Danny.

"OK," said Mum, "I know you're not little any more. And the truth is that even though I'll always worry, I'm really proud of your racing. I know how committed you are to it; I know how much loving care you put into that vehicle. You are so focused and determined when

114

it comes to driving and I think those are qualities that will really help you out in life, and not just with karting."

Danny blushed at this praise.

"Anyway," she continued, "what's happened to your kart is despicable. I'm furious with whoever did it. But that doesn't help matters. So this is what I'm going to do. I'm going to give you your share of the money to repair your kart – if it's possible between now and tomorrow. Dad's mate Spike is Mr Kart Repairs and if there's any chance he can do it, then I think we have to try."

"Julie. . ." said Dad.

"It's fine, Ed," said Mum. "Danny, if you ever get any prize money from karting, you can pay me back and I'll put that money aside for your education. But I know this is your dream so of course I'll help in any way I can."

There was absolute silence round the kitchen table.

"Well?" said Mum, looking at Dad. "Haven't you got a phone call to make?"

As Dad grabbed the phone and dialled Spike's number, Danny threw his arms round Mum, while Katie threw her arms round him again.

"You don't need to do this," said Danny, his heart pounding with the emotion of it all.

"Yes we do," smiled Mum. "Let's just hear what Spike has to say."

The three of them turned towards Dad, who had just got through.

"Spike," he said. "It's Ed Sharp. I've got a bit of a problem. It's Danny's kart. It's been a bit smashed up and he needs it tomorrow for a major race. Is there *any* chance you could take a look at it?"

Danny watched his dad anxiously.

Dad took a deep breath and blew out his cheeks.

Danny grimaced. Had Spike given Dad a no?

Dad nodded several times. "OK," he said. And then he put down the phone.

"What did he say?" asked Danny with huge eyes.

"He's not sure he'll be able to do anything before the race," replied Dad.

Danny's spirits were floored again.

"But he's willing to have a look at it and give it his best shot," added Dad. "So the sooner we get it to him, the better."

It didn't take Danny long to respond. Two seconds later he and Dad were hurrying out of the door, destination Sparks Cross.

"GOOD LUCK!" shouted Mum and Katie, waving them off.

We'll seriously need it, thought Danny, as he and Dad sped out of the close.

19

Danny and Dad made it to Sparks Cross in record time and told Alfie what was going on. Alfie quickly hitched his trailer to Dad's van and helped them load Danny's kart inside. Once that was done, Danny and Dad set off for Spike's repair shop.

The shop was a kart lover's dream. The whole place was covered in karts, pieces of karts and karting accessories. Top-of-the-range body suits, gloves, boots and helmets sat next to books and manuals on driving techniques and skills.

Spike was a large guy with a pot belly and a thin goatee. He shook Dad's hand and then Danny's. "Sorry to hear about your kart," he said. "It was involved in an accident, right?"

"Something like that," replied Danny.

Spike gave him a puzzled look but then he said,

"Come on, let's take a look at it."

They exited the shop and Spike leant over the side of the trailer to check out the vehicle. He tutted to himself several times as he took in the kart's situation.

"And this race is tomorrow, right?"

Danny and Dad both nodded.

"OK," said Spike. "I'll take a proper look at her in the workshop and see what I can do. But I can't promise anything. You might need a miracle and I'm no miracle maker. I suggest you go home and I'll phone you later."

Danny's dad patted Spike on the shoulder. "You're a real mate," he said gratefully.

"No worries," replied Spike. "You've helped me out in the past, Ed. I'll be in touch."

Danny couldn't sit still on the journey home. His feet were tapping up and down; his fists were clenching and unclenching. "Do you think he'll be able to do it by tomorrow?" he asked repeatedly.

"You heard what he said; he'll do his best. But time's not on our side."

The whole thing still seemed so unreal to Danny. He was certain the smashed kart was the handiwork of Tony Butler – the guy was a complete nutcase. How good would it be if Spike could fix up the kart and Danny could take on Tony in the race and beat him? But was this a realistic possibility now? Spike had said he wasn't a miracle maker, so Danny knew he needed to prepare himself for major disappointment. And there was no way he was going to drive the quarter-final in a club kart; he'd be consumed alive by the other drivers.

Back at home, Mum made hot chocolate for them all and Katie handed Danny a drawing. "This is for you," she said.

It was of a race track. There were several small karts on the track but at the front of the pack was a massive one: Danny's. There were fireworks going off all around the track, in blues and reds and greens.

Danny felt choked up and gave his kid sister a big side hug. "It's fantastic, Katie!" he said. "Thanks."

Katie was chuffed. "I bet Spike will make your kart even *better* than it was before those horrible people smashed it up," she said.

Danny smiled but he didn't quite agree with her theory.

But after the hot chocolate was downed and Katie had been packed off to bed, Danny's nerves kicked back in. He paced around the kitchen. How was he going to get through the next twelve hours, not knowing if Spike could do anything for his kart?

"You're driving me mad," said Dad after a while. "Stomping round in circles isn't going to do you any good. You need to build up some strength for tomorrow."

"I can't help it," replied Danny testily.

"Look," said Mum, walking over to him. "Why don't you go on that computer racing game of yours for a bit you know, take your mind off things?"

Danny stopped pacing. That wasn't a bad idea.

He went to his room and switched on *Power Wheels 7*.

His mind was so stretched by the day's events that at first he couldn't get into it, but after a while he managed to lose himself in the virtual action. In a twenty-lap race, he missed out on beating Le Grand by a couple of seconds. It wasn't a victory, but he knew that every day he was getting closer to finally beating the Frenchman.

But his small sense of satisfaction with his computer game skills was diverted when he heard the phone ring. He ran down to the kitchen.

Dad had the receiver in his hand. "It's Spike," he mouthed.

Danny felt waves of anxiety wash through him as Dad listened to what Spike had to say with a very serious expression on his face. When the call was over, Dad despondently replaced the receiver.

"It doesn't look good," he said slowly.

Danny's heart plummeted. "What did he say?"

"The damage to the chassis is pretty serious and the brakes are a mess. He's got to deal with a customer for the next couple of hours and then he'll start on your kart.

It'll mean him working well into the night. It's pretty amazing of him. He'll see what he can do."

But Danny couldn't really think about how amazing Spike Thomas was. He well knew the adult phrase, "*He'll see what he can do.*" It normally meant absolutely nothing could be done. All he could think of was the fact that tomorrow, when the Granger Cup quarter-final was taking place, he wouldn't be one of the drivers. It was that simple – his dream of glory, along with his kart, had been fatally crushed.

20

Danny's eyes sprung open. He looked at the time on his bedside clock: 7.51 a.m.; He ran downstairs and checked the answerphone. The blinking red light was off. This wasn't good. No cheery message from Spike saying his kart was as good as new. He ran to the kitchen table, where Dad always left his phone, and checked it for messages; again, nothing. He sat down and put his head in his hands. It was unbelievable; all of that practice, all of that commitment, and he wouldn't be able to show anyone what he was capable of.

A thud on the doormat announced the arrival of the newspaper. Danny considered leaving it, but as there was nothing better to do, he went to retrieve it. He flipped straight to the back for the sports coverage. Cricket dominated the first few pages, followed by tennis and golf. At last he found a small piece about Formula One, but it was just about weather conditions for the upcoming Hungarian Grand Prix. However, at the bottom of the column was a large, bold statement directing the reader to page four for a "Top Formula One Story".

Danny sighed; it was bound to be something about sponsorship or new TV coverage – those were the sort of Formula One stories that usually made the news pages. He flicked unenthusiastically to page four.

FORMULA ONE STAR BLOCKS REPORTER'S "SMEAR STORY"

Late last night, up and coming Formula One ace Scot Devlin managed to get an eleventh-hour injunction to stop a piece by the so-called "Attack Dog" – reporter Vince Dutton – appearing in today's Daily News*. Devlin received a tip-off that the* News *was going to run with a story about his alleged involvement with an illegal financial scam. Devlin's lawyer, Angela Banks, stated that even though the nature of Dutton's "manifestly untrue" allegations were already widely known within the sporting world, to release such a story in the national press would defame her client and incur loss of future earnings. Miss Banks added that the documents Dutton intended to use were known only to her and Devlin – the suggestion being that Mr*

Dutton obtained them by foul means. When contacted, Mr Dutton refused to answer questions about the injunction, other than to say that he was sticking by his story. Miss Banks said that Devlin is considering all of his options in relation to Dutton's actions and that she will be making an announcement in the next couple of days.

Danny read the article three times before putting the newspaper down. So his plan had worked. The "tip-off" had been from him! If he hadn't gone to Devlin's pad and handed that note over, Dutton's story would have appeared in the papers today, catching an unsuspecting Scot Devlin totally off guard. Maybe now Devlin would forget about Danny's overstepping the mark at Malloy HQ?

A few seconds later he heard the guttural sound of a truck driving into the close.

He ran to the window and threw open the curtains. A huge red lorry was double parking outside the house, and there, stepping down from the driver's door, was Spike Thomas.

Danny raced outside. Spike was just starting to lower the back of the truck.

"Danny!" shouted Spike. "Just stand back a minute and let me get her down off the ramp."

Danny watched with bated breath as the ramp at the back of the truck hit the pavement. Spike jumped up and carefully directed Danny's kart down the slope and on to the tarmac. Danny felt like he was watching a TV illusion. There was his kart, but the dents and twists had been smoothed out, like a pair of large, badly creased trousers that had just been ironed. The brakes had been fixed and looked in great shape.

Danny's dad, who'd been woken by the truck, came out of the house in his dressing gown; he also looked at the kart in amazement.

"Hey, guys," said Spike. "I know it looks the part – and believe me it took a while to make it look this way – but if I'm really honest with you, this isn't much more than a patch-up job."

"When you say a patch-up job, what do you mean?" asked Dad.

Spike wrinkled his nose. "The kart will be good for today's race. Danny will be able to put it through its paces and drive very competitively, without any danger to himself or the vehicle. But I'm afraid that will be it. The best I can do is a one-race fix. If you wanted to compete in it after that, you'd need to spend hundreds and hundreds of pounds. I'm really sorry, but that's the way it is."

Danny's joy at getting his kart back in a fit state to race was countered by his despair that it wouldn't be racing again. Mum was using her "education fund" to pay Spike for the repairs. Now that there was nothing left, there was no way he'd be able to get a decent second-hand kart, let alone a new one. And with twenty out of twenty rejection letters, there wasn't going to be any pile of cash heading their way in the foreseeable future. He'd probably have to wait years for a chance to get his hands on a half-decent vehicle again.

Dad went back into the house and Mum came out clutching a wad of notes. "Here," she said, handing them over to Spike.

Spike looked embarrassed. "Julie . . . look . . . I feel bad about taking this, I. . ."

"Take it," she insisted, "you've more than earned it. We'll be forever grateful for what you've done."

Spike sighed and took the money. He gave Danny's hand a very firm shake.

"Thanks, Spike," said Danny gratefully. "You've done an amazing job!"

"Only tell me that when you win the race," grinned Spike, before lifting the ramp and closing up the back of the truck. He climbed into the driver's cab and gunned the engine. Mum, Katie, Danny and Dad stood in the street waving him off until the red truck had vanished from view.

The next hour was a complete blur. Danny grabbed some breakfast, had a shower and got all his karting gear together.

At 9.45, Dad announced it was time to make a move. He and Danny loaded the kart into Dad's trailer and set off for Sparks Cross. The race began at twelve p.m. They'd have plenty of time to get prepared.

Mum and Katie came out to wave them off.

"You will be extra careful in the race today, won't you?" asked Mum, looking anxious.

"Of course I will," Danny smiled. "I always am."

"Well then, good luck," said Mum.

"Cheers," replied Danny, "and thank you SO MUCH for paying for the repairs. I can only race today because of you!"

"It's a pleasure," smiled Mum. "Now go out there and give it your best shot, kiddo!"

On the journey, Danny was a jumble of thoughts and emotions, but he knew he had to try and clear his mind and focus on one thing only: the race.

"We'll be there soon," said Dad, glancing sideways at his son and seeing the anxious expression on his face. "And above all, go out there and enjoy it, mate. You've dealt really well with having your kart damaged so badly. Now you're back in the race, just go for it. I know you can qualify for the semi-finals."

For the last fifteen minutes of the journey, Danny went over all of his race preparations. If this was going to be his last race in his beloved kart, then he was determined to make it the race of his life.

But as soon as Dad pulled into the road leading down to Sparks Cross, Danny felt an extra tightening in his chest, and it wasn't just pre-race nerves. It was the sound; the sound of karts racing. And as the track came into view it was clear that this wasn't just a practice session.

This was the real thing.

The Granger Cup Quarter-Final was already under way.

21

Danny and his father looked at each other, aghast.

"What the hell..." Danny's words dissolved into the void of shock they both felt.

They got out of the car in stunned silence.

"Why didn't anyone tell me the start time had moved?" asked Danny incredulously, furious that after all of the efforts he, Dad and Spike had made to get his kart race-ready, he'd now missed his chance to progress to the semis.

But at that moment, Alfie Price emerged from his office and began striding towards them.

"It's OK," he shouted when he got within earshot. "It's not what you think."

"It looks like it!" replied Danny.

"It's not the Granger Cup race," explained Alfie, as he reached them. "The Viking Road Kart Club have had a lot of problems with their track and it's unraceable today. They asked us if we could stage a race for them, so that's what's going on. The Granger Cup heat is still at twelve."

Danny had never felt so relieved in his life.

"We thought we'd missed it," said Dad, who looked incredibly relieved too.

"I take it that Spike was able to knock your kart into shape then?" asked Alfie.

Danny nodded. "He did an incredible job; got it back to us early this morning. It'll be fine for the race but Spike said that would probably be the end of its career."

Alfie's face fell. "I'm sorry to hear that. And I'm still fuming about the vandals who did this."

"Me too," nodded Dad.

Tony Butler, thought Danny.

Alfie quickly focused on the present. "Right, you two get sorted," he said in a businesslike fashion, "and I'll see you in a bit."

As Alfie hurried back to his office, Danny and Dad began easing the kart off the trailer. As they were doing this, a car pulled up beside them. In the driving seat was Tony Butler's dad. In the passenger seat was Tony Butler. He was staring in open-eyed shock at the state of Danny's kart.

The look on his face was proof that Tony had committed the crime. He was dumbfounded by the kart's transformation. Danny was suddenly overcome by the urge to grab Tony by the collar and drag him out through the open window of the car. He'd nearly destroyed Danny's racing dreams. And even though Danny could drive today, Tony's handiwork had ensured the end of the kart's life. That was a terrible thing to have done.

But before Danny could act on his impulse, Tony's dad drove off to find a parking space.

"Are you OK, Danny?" asked Dad.

Danny's eyes followed Tony and his dad for a few moments and then he snapped back to the present. "Yeah, I'm fine. Let's get the kart over to the track."

The Viking Road race was coming to an end. The drivers who'd finished were nudging their karts to the side of the track, stopping and dismounting. Danny had a quick glance at his watch: eleven o'clock.

The Granger Cup Quarter-Final was in one hour.

He felt his nerves ratchet up a notch. He had his kart back – this was good. But what would happen if he didn't make it through to the semis, and Tony, with his brand new kart, did?

He pushed these thoughts to the back of his mind and concentrated on wheeling his kart to the side of the track. Lots of the other drivers were already there, most of them with one or both parents beside them. Danny recognized a few faces from other events and he exchanged some hellos, but there were lots he'd never

seen before. That was the thing about the Granger Cup –
it brought in people from a really large area. Tony was
there with his dad, working on his gleaming kart. Danny
felt a pang of jealousy over the newness and great spec
of the kart.

Forget it, he ordered himself.

"Just remember everything you've learned," said Dad,
putting an arm round his son's shoulders. "All the tips
and tricks you've picked up. Drive like you normally do
and you'll do well."

Danny swallowed nervously. By now, all of the drivers
in the previous race had vacated the track. Danny chatted
to a couple of the drivers he recognized from that race.
Then he crouched down over his kart and he and Dad
worked on last-minute tweaks.

A short while later several men wearing fluorescent
jackets spread themselves around the track – the race
marshals. These guys were paid from the money that
Danny and the other drivers paid to take part in the race.
The marshals were the ones who had the power to stop
drivers behind an out-of-control kart or an accident, and
they also had the power to completely stop a race by
waving a red flag. Every marshal wore an earpiece and
mike so that they could communicate with one another
and the clerk. Alfie was the Granger Cup Quarter-Final
race clerk – he was in overall control of all the marshals

and drivers. He walked over in the direction of Danny and his co-riders, carrying a clipboard.

"OK," announced Alfie. "This is for all of you who are going to be racing in the Granger Cup Quarter-Final."

Danny and the eleven other drivers stopped what they were doing and faced Alfie. "There's going to be a three-lap practice session," Alfie declared, "and then we're having a rolling start. Your position on the grid has been determined by how many points you've accumulated in your club's championships so far this season."

Alfie pulled twelve sheets off his clipboard and handed one to every driver. Danny quickly studied his. He was seventh on the grid. Tony Butler was an intimidating third. Danny's stomach wobbled – Tony was starting with a big advantage over him. Pole position was given to a red and white kart driven by a lad named Kai. Danny had seen him race once before – he was excellent and fully deserved the number one spot.

"The practice laps will start in five minutes," announced Alfie. "Walking pace with no overtaking, everyone got that?"

Twelve drivers, including Danny, nodded.

"As you all know, the actual race will be twelve laps," added Alfie, "so don't go burning too much adrenaline before you get going. First three places qualify for the semis."

A few minutes later, Danny and Dad pushed his kart on to the track, where the drivers were lining up in twos. A man with shaved hair and a green karting suit was acting as scrutineer for the race day. His job was to make sure that all karts were racing legitimately – meaning no one had tampered with their engine or made illegal alterations to their vehicle. It was amazing the lengths some pushy parents went to give their kid an (illegal) mechanical advantage. The scrutineer walked between the karts, checking every one, and finally gave a thumbs up to the entire field.

In seventh place, Danny was in the fourth row of two, next to the eighth-placed driver – a tall kid with dark brown hair and twitching eyes. In the second pair up ahead was Tony, with the fourth-placed guy. Danny cast a glance at Tony, who was smiling smugly as he eased his brand new vehicle on to the grid.

Dad handed Danny his gloves. He slipped them on and pulled them until they were comfortable. Then he climbed into the seat and checked all of the instruments. Dad then passed his helmet over. Danny took it and placed it on his head, swivelling it a bit to the left until the fit was right.

"Go for it!" grinned Dad, clenching his fist in a show of support. "Keep your focus, do everything that Alfie has told you and don't think about it being your kart's last race. Live in the moment and have fun – yeah?"

"Totally," nodded Danny with determination on his face.

Alfie waited until all of the drivers were in their karts and then gave a shout for the practice laps to begin. Twelve drivers hit their touch and go buttons and in twos they set off.

Danny drove at a decent pace, looking up for the corner ahead and focusing completely on the interaction between him, his kart and the track. He drove right beside the kid in eighth. Spike had clearly done a good job; the kart was bearing up well. But racing all-out at seventy mph was going to be a different matter. All of the other drivers were playing safe too – nobody wanted to break the speed limit set by Alfie.

At the end of the second lap, Danny was feeling good about his kart. Yes, it was a complete tragedy that this would be its last race, but who knew what he might achieve today.

As the procession of cars headed to the start/finish line at the end of their third lap, one of the marshals held up his green flag and then waved it vigorously.

The Granger Cup Quarter-Final had begun!

22

Danny's start was good. He accelerated quickly, his hands gripping the steering wheel. Within seconds he was braking for the first bend and taking it smoothly on the inside, just ahead of the eighth-placed driver. With twelve whole laps to go, he had to grab one of the top three semi-final berths, and he'd never felt so determined to achieve a goal in his life. Kai's red and white kart held on tightly to pole position.

With the first lap successfully completed, Danny made a break in the middle of the second lap, overtaking the kart in front on an inside bend, putting him in sixth place, with Tony still in third. For the next two laps, the order of vehicles at the front remained unchanged. Danny was delighted his kart was holding up; the adrenaline was rushing through him. If he could hold his nerve and his kart didn't give up on him, he had a chance!

On lap five, Tony overtook the second-placed driver, putting himself in second position; Danny remained in sixth. His kart was now operating at max speed but he felt fully in control, making small adjustments to his braking on the bends. Even though his body was rigid with concentration, he began to relax a little, to enjoy the race.

The spectators – waving and cheering their favoured drivers – were now whooshing by, a series of dots at the side of the track. Danny dropped a couple of miles per hour in speed and then accelerated on the second bend of the sixth lap to overtake the fifth-placed silver kart in front of him, and then the next one – a maroon vehicle. This placed him in fourth position.

He adjusted his body slightly and gazed down the track. With a burst of speed at the next corner, he went outside first and then sharply cut inside, flummoxing the driver in front. Now things were really hotting up. Tony was in second and Danny was in third – both qualification positions. And Tony was there for the taking, new kart or not. Lap eight rushed by. Danny kept calm, plotted his moment.

It came on the final corner of lap nine. Approaching the bend, Danny pulled to the outer side of the track. It was a risky strategy because he could lose control of his kart, but his timing was perfect. As Tony slowed down an extra measure for a smooth corner, Danny accelerated.

Tony was totally unprepared for this and twisted his head in shock when Danny zoomed past him and quickly put some distance between them. Danny was now second; Tony third.

Yes! Danny felt a zinging sensation in his chest; Tony was now behind him, still trying to take in what had just happened. Danny sped on, completing lap nine and even managing to gain ground on Kai's red and white kart.

Danny could feel the elation building up; if he could hang on, he'd be booking a place at the Granger Cup Semis.

But nothing could have prepared him for the event that occurred on the third bend of lap ten. He was so focused on his vehicle and the possibility of overtaking Kai that he had no awareness of a kart edging towards him and then exploding with a burst of speed as it hit the bend. One second, he was driving totally smoothly; the next he felt an almighty crash against the side of his vehicle as Tony Butler thundered past him, knocking him ferociously sideways.

Danny's kart hurtled towards the outer edge of the track, his tyres spinning and screeching as they skidded. His steering wheel jerked violently; he desperately tried to pull it back, without luck. Danny's kart twisted and flew and he felt the terrible sensation that his vehicle was about to take off and flip right over, putting both vehicle and driver in grave danger.

23

Immediately the marshal at the next marshal station raised his yellow flag, which instructed drivers that there was to be no overtaking behind Danny, because he was in trouble. One of the marshals immediately alerted the ambulance station in case Danny got injured. Kai and Tony didn't have to worry about this; the next yellow flag stayed down so they could speed on.

Danny's senses were in overload as his right-side wheels left the ground. All awareness of the other karts vanished as he fought to regain control of his vehicle. As the right-hand side of the kart started to tip, Danny leant down hard left and slammed his foot down on the brake. The kart wavered madly for a split second and then crashed back down on to the track.

Danny's survival instinct and emergency manoeuvre had saved him. It was incredible that he'd averted a hideous smash-up. The yellow flag was lowered and three vehicles quickly overtook him as he swerved back on to the track; he was now back in sixth position. Fury at Tony Butler pounded in his brain. He hoped one of the marshals had seen exactly what had happened. Tony was bound to be called in for a "judicial" in the office after the race with the race officials.

At the start of lap eleven, Danny was feeling dejected and cheated, but a steel core of determination still pulsed through him. He had just two laps to make it into the semis – was there any way he could do it? He powered forward, desperately hoping for a break. It came on the final bend of lap eleven; the two cars in front of him both went outside. Alfie's words about looking at the gap, not the kart, came flooding back, and he snatched the inside and the momentum; fourth place was his. But he still had loads to do.

He entered the twelfth and final lap and took a quick glance at the side of the track. To his utter astonishment he spotted Mum and Katie. They were standing by Dad's side and were cheering Danny on. Mum had come to a race and brought Katie – he couldn't believe it! She must have seen the smash with Tony – not a soothing thing to calm her nerves at her first race meeting. But the sight of her and Katie spurred Danny on even further. It was the first time they'd ever seen him race, so he wanted to make them proud.

He faced front with renewed determination, accelerated and quickly managed to draw level with the kart in front. Switching from outside to inside, he shot forward and tried to overtake it on the second straight, but the third-placed driver wasn't having it. He blocked Danny's efforts and Danny shouted with frustration.

He pressed his foot down as hard as it would go on the accelerator in an attempt to squeeze that tiny bit of extra thrust out of his kart. He bolted to the left. The third-placed kart matched his move and blocked him again. Danny tried going right – once again the kart in front mirrored his move. How on earth was he going to get through?

With three hundred metres to go, he was out of the qualification places. If Tony hadn't deliberately smashed into him, the story would be so different. But with just two hundred metres to go, Danny saw an opportunity. The kart in front braked heavily going into the penultimate bend. Danny knew a chance when he saw one and seized it. Instead of braking, he kept going at phenomenal speed. As he entered the bend, the kart in front cut inside, presuming this would put a barrier up to Danny's progress, but Danny went outside. His sheer speed saw him whoosh forward and burn up his rival. He was in third place again – back in the qualification positions!

But this wasn't enough for Danny. He had to beat Tony

Butler. And he had to do it quickly. There was no way he was going to let a nutcase cheater beat him.

Tony went inside on the final bend of lap twelve. Danny went outside. As they exited the bend, Danny turned his wheel hard left. Tony tried to block him by going left too, but Danny was too quick for him. With fearsome velocity, Danny hurtled past Tony into second place.

Incredible!

Desperately, Tony tried to make up ground, but Danny had pulled away. He was too far ahead now. The final straight loomed up and the race leader, Kai, shot down it, crossing the line in first place. Tony made a last-gasp bid to steal back second place but Danny held firm and flew across the line a metre ahead of his arch enemy.

He'd done it. He'd qualified for the Granger Cup Semis *and* beaten Tony!

Danny laughed, steered the kart to the edge of the track and climbed out of the seat. He felt a surge of exhilaration. It was easily the best race he'd ever run. He knew it was a massive achievement. A few metres away, Tony Butler pulled his gleaming kart off the track, got out and raised his fists in the air, in celebration.

Danny was about to run over and confront Tony, but Alfie Price got in there first.

"What did you think you were doing out there?"

shouted Alfie in Tony's face.

"It was an accident!" protested Tony, taking off his helmet and trying to look as innocent as possible.

"It didn't look like one to me!" snarled Alfie. "It looked like a deliberate attack. I'll see you in the clerk's office in ten minutes!"

"I said it was an accident!" wailed Tony, but Alfie's face was resolute; he would be speaking to all of the marshals who'd seen the incident and firmly quizzing Tony in a judicial. He might even disqualify him.

At that moment Katie ran over to Danny and threw herself at him. "That was AMAZING!" she shouted. "You were so FAST at the end when you overtook that other kart. I can't WAIT till I can get out there on the track. It's going to be SO awesome!"

Danny laughed.

"You were superb!" grinned Mum. "Really impressive."

"What made you come to the race?" asked Danny, still amazed that she and Katie were there.

"What with your kart being smashed up and everything, I really felt I had to come," she explained. "I knew how big today was for you and I knew how much you'd gone through just to get here. I won't say I wasn't nervous, and when your kart was nearly knocked off the track I had visions of air ambulances and terrible injuries. But you pulled it round, you got back into it and then you managed to finish second. It was fantastic!"

She hugged him tightly.

"Do you think Tony Butler deliberately tried to force you off the track?" asked Dad, joining them.

"Maybe," said Danny with a shrug of his shoulders, knowing full well what Tony's intention had been. Once again, the facts about Danny's kart hit him.

"It doesn't matter about Tony," said Danny, his expression suddenly forlorn. "I may have made it to the semis, but I won't be able to drive in them."

"But there's something I need to tell you," said Mum, reaching into her coat pocket.

At that second Danny's mobile went.

UNKNOWN CALLER read the display.

Danny pressed ACCEPT. "Hello?"

"Hello Danny. It's Scot Devlin."

24

Danny's heart stopped beating for a second. His instant thought was that it was Carl having a laugh. But the voice sounded remarkably like Devlin's and Carl wasn't a great impersonator.

"Danny. Are you there?"

"I'm here." Danny took a few steps away from his family. His mum had got some piece of paper in her hands, his dad was looking angry about Tony's tricks and Katie was just swept up in the excitement of the moment.

"Look," said Devlin, "I'm sorry Bill Moore was harsh with you at the track the other day. We've all been young; we've all said things that might be taken as arrogant."

"So . . . so . . . you weren't offended?" asked Danny.

"It takes a lot more to offend me than that," laughed Devlin, "and I don't reckon Bill thinks it's such a big deal. He used to be a teacher – he was just being teacher-y with you."

Danny let out a long breath of relief.

"Anyway," went on Devlin, "I got your number off Bill and I'm phoning for two reasons."

"Yes?"

"First there's the matter of the note you got to me," said Devlin. "That was an incredibly determined and decent thing to do and it helped me immensely. If you hadn't taken the time and effort to let me know about Vince Dutton and his disgraceful antics, a newspaper might have printed his story. If that had happened, people would have said there's no smoke without fire, and my sponsors might have begun to view me as a tainted brand. You saved my reputation. I owe you for that."

Danny was delighted with the way the call was going. "What was the second thing?" he asked.

"I want you to come back to Malloy HQ and spend some time with me. Like I said, you remind me of myself at your age and I could have really done with some input from a real driver back then. I *am* a real driver and I reckon I can help you out – if you're up for it?"

"Totally!" gushed Danny, completely exhilarated.

"Excellent," replied Devlin. "I'll get Bill to set it all up."

"That would be amazing!" cried Danny.

"I'll see you around, then!" said Devlin.

And suddenly the call was over. Danny's thrill at the remarkable conversation didn't last long, though, because his mind snapped straight back to his kart, or rather his lack of one. Scot Devlin had said he was going to teach him some stuff, but without a kart, Danny wouldn't be able to do any racing. It was an agonizing situation.

He was so engrossed in these thoughts that at first he didn't hear his name being said.

"Danny." It was Mum.

He tuned out of his head and into her voice. "Danny," she said, "I think you and Dad should take a look at this. It came after you left. It's from one of the sponsors Dad wrote to. It was addressed to Dad but I recognized the address it came from so I had to open it. Here."

She handed Danny the piece of paper she was clutching. It was a letter. Danny looked down at it. Dad stood over his shoulder and read it at the same time.

Frank Hoult
Managing Director
Point Power Electronics

Dear Mr Sharp

I have recently taken over as MD of Point Power Electronics and am very keen to involve the company with outside projects, both to build our brand and to support different members of the community, especially in the world of sport. One of my team leaders mentioned the fact that you'd written to us seeking sponsorship for your son, Danny and that we'd turned you down. I understand he is a very talented karter and has aspirations to rise through the ranks up to Formula One.

As a keen Formula One aficionado, I'd very much like to meet you and Danny. Obviously I can't give you any guarantees at this stage, but having seen the history of Danny's karting career to date, I was very impressed. I believe that this is exactly the kind of project I'd like the company to be involved with. Please call me on my work number or my mobile, both of which are listed below.

I look forward to meeting you both and wish Danny the best of luck with his current karting commitments.

Yours sincerely
Frank Holt

Danny looked up and in an instant he and Dad were jumping around like two crazed toddlers who'd just been given a giant barrel filled to the brim with chocolate.

25

It took Danny and Dad quite a while to calm down.

"Does this mean Danny can carry on racing?" asked Katie.

"It might well do," smiled Dad. "We'll set up a meeting with Mr Holt and see what he has to say."

"What a completely mad twenty-four hours," laughed Mum. "I'm so thrilled for you, Danny. You deserve all of the good luck you can get."

Danny grinned. He hadn't even told his family about his phone call with Scot Devlin. He'd tell them later – when everything was a bit calmer.

"Right," said Mum. "I'm taking Katie into town to buy some new clothes. We'll see you back at home later. And well done again, Danny – I'm so proud of you."

"Oh please, Mum!" wailed Katie. "This is the first time

you've let me come to the track. Let me stay a little bit longer!"

"Now we've been here once, we'll come again," replied Mum, "but one of our jobs today is to get you clothes. So come on!"

Katie sighed with deep disappointment, gave Danny another hug and traipsed off after Mum. Dad went off to talk to Alfie, and Danny was about to go and hang out with some of the other drivers when Tony Butler sauntered over.

"You were lucky," sneered Tony. "Next time you won't be."

"And you were well out of order!" shouted Danny. "You could have killed me!"

"Don't be pathetic," snorted Tony derisively. "I hardly touched you."

"Well, let's see what happens at the judicial," said Danny.

"Nothing will happen!" snapped Tony.

"Yeah, right!" snarled Danny. "Your problem is that you can't stand being beaten. Just like on the basketball court. If things don't go your way, you cheat and then sulk like a baby."

Tony's easy-going expression hardened to one of outright contempt. "You'll regret saying that," he hissed.

"Yeah, yeah," said Danny, buoyed both by his

performance on the track and the contents of the letter he'd just read.

"Anyway," said Tony, regaining his hostile composure, "it doesn't matter about you qualifying for the semis. I heard Alfie Price saying that this was the last race your kart would run. So I guess it's back to racing the club karts for you. You won't stand a chance in the semis."

But instead of pulling the offended scowl that Tony expected, Danny burst out laughing. Tony stared at him with disbelief.

"What's so funny?" asked a confused Tony.

But Danny had already turned his back on Tony and was walking away. With a potential sponsor and Scot Devlin acting as his personal coach, his racing career was far from over. In fact, without a shadow of doubt, Danny Sharp would be back!

Acknowledgements

Thanks to: Colin Wright and family for their amazing trackside hospitality (including David Wright – a real-life Danny Sharp!) and to Colin for his forensic knowledge of karts and the karting world; Nick Reid for his fact-checking and brilliant insights about Formula 1; Zöe Duncan, for being such an excellent editor and a great person to work with; and Stephanie Thwaites, agent supreme!

Jonny Zucker worked as a teacher and stand-up comedian before turning to writing full-time. He has now written over thirty books for children, teenagers and adults. Jonny became a fan of Formula One at a young age and first drove a kart at the age of eight. Jonny has always wanted to bring the excitement and nail-biting tension of racing to readers, and is pleased he can do this through Danny Sharp. Jonny lives with his wife and three young children in North London.